THIS DIARY BELONGS TO:

Nikki J. Maxwell

PRIVATE & CONFIDENTIAL

If found, please return to ME for REWARD!

(NO SNOOPING ALLOWED!!!☹)

ALSO BY
Rachel Renée Russell

Coming soon!
the misadventures of MAX CRUMBLY

Rachel Renée Russell

DORK diaries

Tales from a NOT-SO- Perfect Pet Sitter

with Nikki Russell and Erin Russell

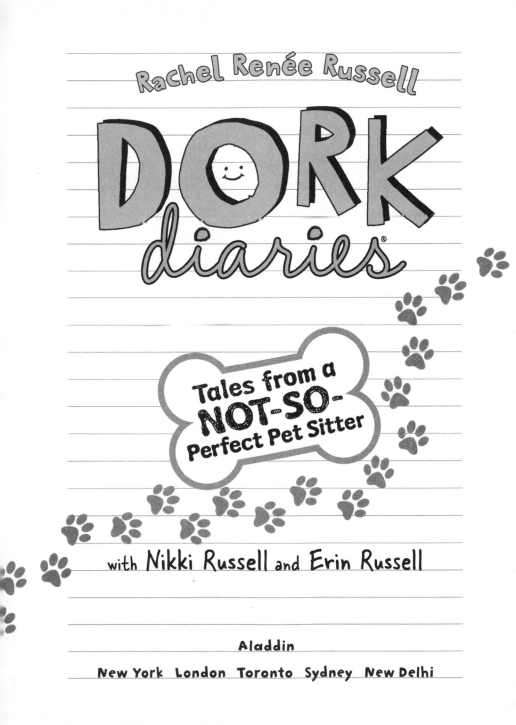

Aladdin

New York London Toronto Sydney New Delhi

ALADDIN * An imprint of Simon & Schuster Children's Publishing Division * 1230 Avenue of the Americas, New York, NY 10020 * First Aladdin hardcover edition October 2015 * Copyright © 2015 by Rachel Renée Russell * All rights reserved, including the right of reproduction in whole or in part in any form. * ALADDIN is a trademark of Simon & Schuster, Inc., and related logo is a registered trademark of Simon & Schuster, Inc. * DORK DIARIES is a registered trademark of Rachel Renée Russell * For information about special discounts for bulk purchases, please contact Simon & Schuster Special Sales at 1-866-506-1949 or business@simonandschuster.com. * The Simon & Schuster Speakers Bureau can bring authors to your live event. For more information or to book an event contact the Simon & Schuster Speakers Bureau at 1-866-248-3049 or visit our website at www.simonspeakers.com. * Series design by Lisa Vega * Cover design by Karin Paprocki * The text of this book was set in Skippy Sharp. * Manufactured in the United States of America 0915 FFG * 10 9 8 7 6 5 4 3 2 1 * This book has been cataloged with the Library of Congress. * ISBN 978-1-4814-5704-0 (POB) * ISBN 978-1-4814-5705-7 (eBook)

In loving memory of
my dad and hero,
Oliver

Thank you for teaching me
to dream big, work hard, and
NEVER give up!

ACKNOWLEDGMENTS

SQUEEEE! We've done it again! I'm thrilled to be adding yet another Dork Diaries book to our wonderful series.

With each and every book, we keep bringing more fun, drama, and excitement from Nikki Maxwell's wacky world.

None of this would have been possible without the support of the following members of TEAM DORK:

Liesa Abrams Mignogna, my SUPERCOOL and CREATIVE editorial director. Thank you for everything that you do! I'm always amazed at how you manage all the moving parts to bring this manuscript in under deadline. I have so much fun working with you. Knowing you're still laughing out loud after reading my books inspires me to continue to share Nikki's voice with the world. I can't wait to introduce our ADORKABLE fans to MAX CRUMBLY and create even more incredible memories with you!

Karin Paprocki, my TALENTED art director. I LOVE LOVE LOVE our puppy paw print book cover! You've produced yet another awesome cover that is sure to be a favorite. Thank you for your AMAZING art direction and for juggling AND surviving our CRAZY schedule.

My wonderful managing editor, Katherine Devendorf. Thank you for your hard work on this series and for hanging out with us into the wee hours of the night. Your efforts have helped us finish yet another awesome book.

Daniel Lazar, my FABULOUS agent at Writers House. Thank you for your honesty and support. You're more than an agent, you're a true friend and die-hard Dork champion. Thanks for believing in me!

A special thanks to my Team Dork staff at Aladdin/ Simon & Schuster: Mara Anastas, Mary Marotta, Jon Anderson, Julie Doebler, Jennifer Romanello, Faye Bi, Carolyn Swerdloff, Lucille Rettino, Matt Pantoliano, Teresa Ronquillo, Michelle Leo, Candace McManus, Anthony Parisi, Christina Pecorale, Gary Urda, and the entire sales force. There's no way I could have done this without you! You're the BEST ever!

To Torie Doherty-Munro at Writers House; to my foreign rights agents Maja Nikolic, Cecilia de la Campa, and Angharad Kowal; and to Deena, Zoé, Marie, and Joy—thanks for helping me Dorkify the world!

Erin, my supertalented coauthor, and Nikki, my supertalented illustrator. I feel so BLESSED to be your mother. Kim, Don, Doris, and my entire family—I am so happy to be sharing this dream with you! I love you all dearly!

Always remember to let your inner DORK shine through!

Okay, I've tried REALLY hard to be polite about all of this! But . . . SORRY!! I JUST CAN'T TAKE IT ANYMORE!!

If I hear MacKenzie Hollister's name one more time, I'm going to . . . SCREAM!!!

I can't believe everyone at this school is STILL talking about her. It's like they're obsessed or something!

"If MacKenzie were here, she'd LOVE this!"

"If MacKenzie were here, she'd HATE that!"

"This school will never be the same without MacKenzie!"

"OMG! I miss MacKenzie SO much!"

MACKENZIE! MACKENZIE! MACKENZIE ☹!!

ME, HAVING A COMPLETE NERVOUS
BREAKDOWN BECAUSE I'M SO SICK OF
EVERYONE TALKING ABOUT MACKENZIE!

Listen up, people! MacKenzie's been GONE for an entire week, and she's NOT coming back!!

So cry yourself a river, build a bridge, and get over it already!!

Okay, I'll admit it.

I was as shocked and surprised as everyone else when she left so abruptly.

But MacKenzie HATED MY GUTS and made my life totally MISERABLE.

And, to be honest, it seems like she's STILL here.

I know this sounds weird, but it's almost like I can FEEL her presence even now as I'm writing in my diary.

But that's probably because the TACKY JUNK kids are leaving for her IS HOGGING UP ALL THE SPACE AT MY LOCKER ☺!!!!

ME, TOTALLY DISGUSTED BY THE JUNK
HOGGING UP MY SPACE ☹!!

I'm sure she's LOVING that her former ex-BFF, Jessica, turned her empty locker into a "We Miss You, MacKenzie!!" shrine, complete with its own Facebook page!

PUH-LEEZE!!

It's obvious to me that MacKenzie is STILL manipulating students.

Especially after that very pathetic and overdramatic FAREWELL LETTER she e-mailed to our school newspaper this morning.

The editor actually published it online for the entire school to read.

OMG! MacKenzie went on and on about how she was tired of the needless suffering and had decided to end it all by moving on to a much better place.

I'm sure she said all that stuff to make everyone feel SORRY for her.

Just in case I decide to EXPOSE all the TERRIBLE things she did before she left.

Just thinking about all this is making me so ANGRY I could chew . . . ROCKS ☹!!

I know I probably shouldn't say this, because it's kind of rude. MacKenzie reminds me of one of those disposable baby diapers!! Why?

THEY'RE BOTH PLASTIC,
TOTALLY SELF-ABSORBED,
AND FULL OF POOP!!

I STILL haven't gotten over all the mean stuff MacKenzie did. Like stealing my diary, breaking into my Miss Know-It-All website, sending really mean fake advice letters to students, and spreading lies and nasty rumors.

And now SHE'S playing the victim just because of a silly video someone sent around of her freaking out over a bug in her hair?! Yeah, right!

Anyway, MacKenzie ended her so-called suffering at Westchester Country Day Middle School by moving on to a so-called better place. . . .

Namely, North Hampton Hills International Academy!

It's a really posh prep school for the children of celebs, politicians, business tycoons, and royalty. Although, now that I think about it, MacKenzie just might fit in with the royalty at that school.

Because she's the biggest DRAMA QUEEN in the history of the universe ☹!! . . .

MACKENZIE, THE DRAMA QUEEN!

Everyone is also RAVING about her new school.

According to MacKenzie, it has a French chef, a Starbucks, riding stables, a spa, a helicopter landing pad, and a plaza of designer boutiques so kids can shop during lunch and after school hours.

And get this! She said her school has ATM machines in every hall, right next to drinking fountains that dispense seven different fruit-flavored waters.

But MacKenzie is such a pathological LIAR, I was starting to wonder if her FAB school even existed.

I wouldn't have been a bit surprised if she'd completely made it up just to impress everyone, when she's really being homeschooled.

So I googled the school and actually found its official website.

OMG! I could NOT believe my eyes! . . .

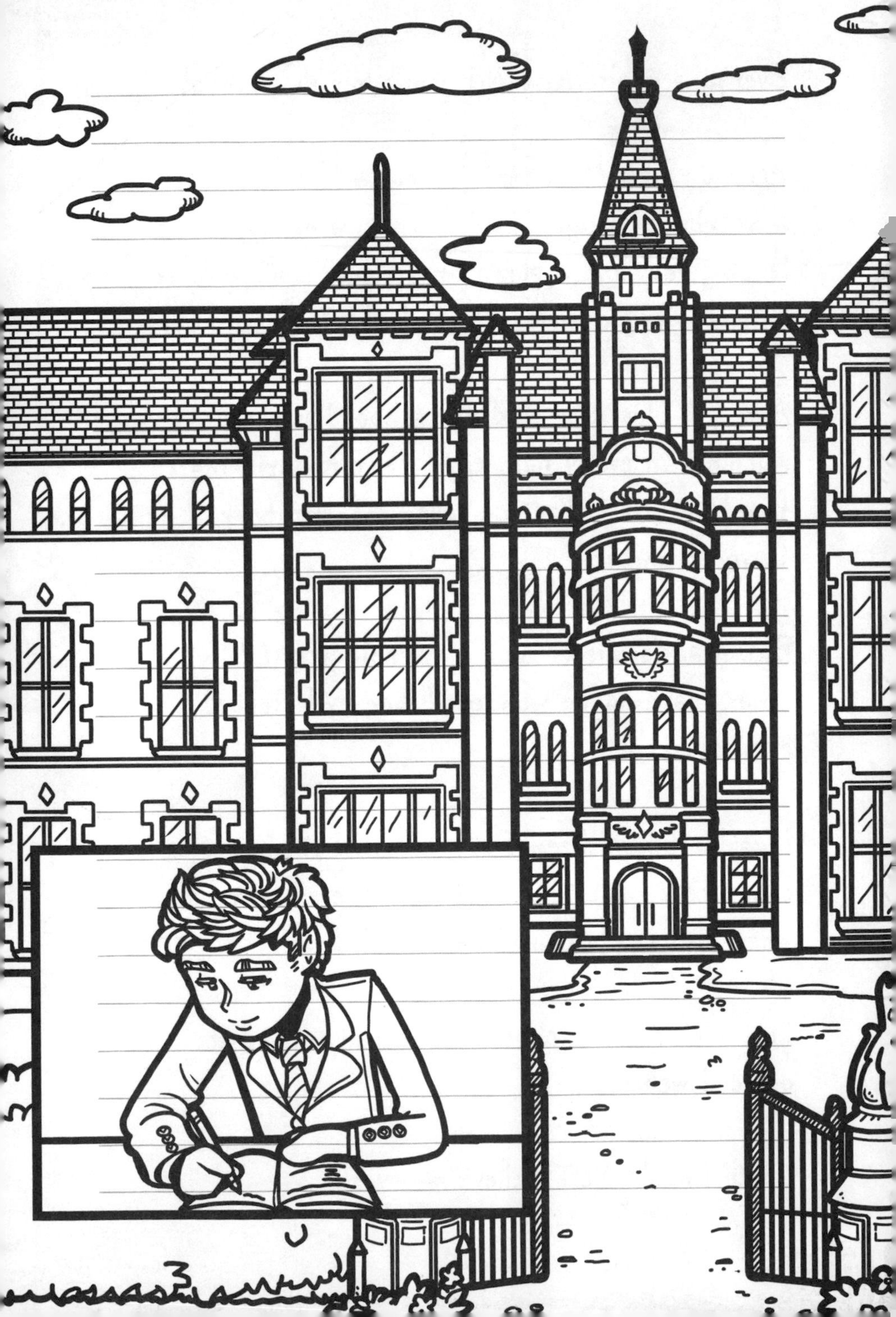

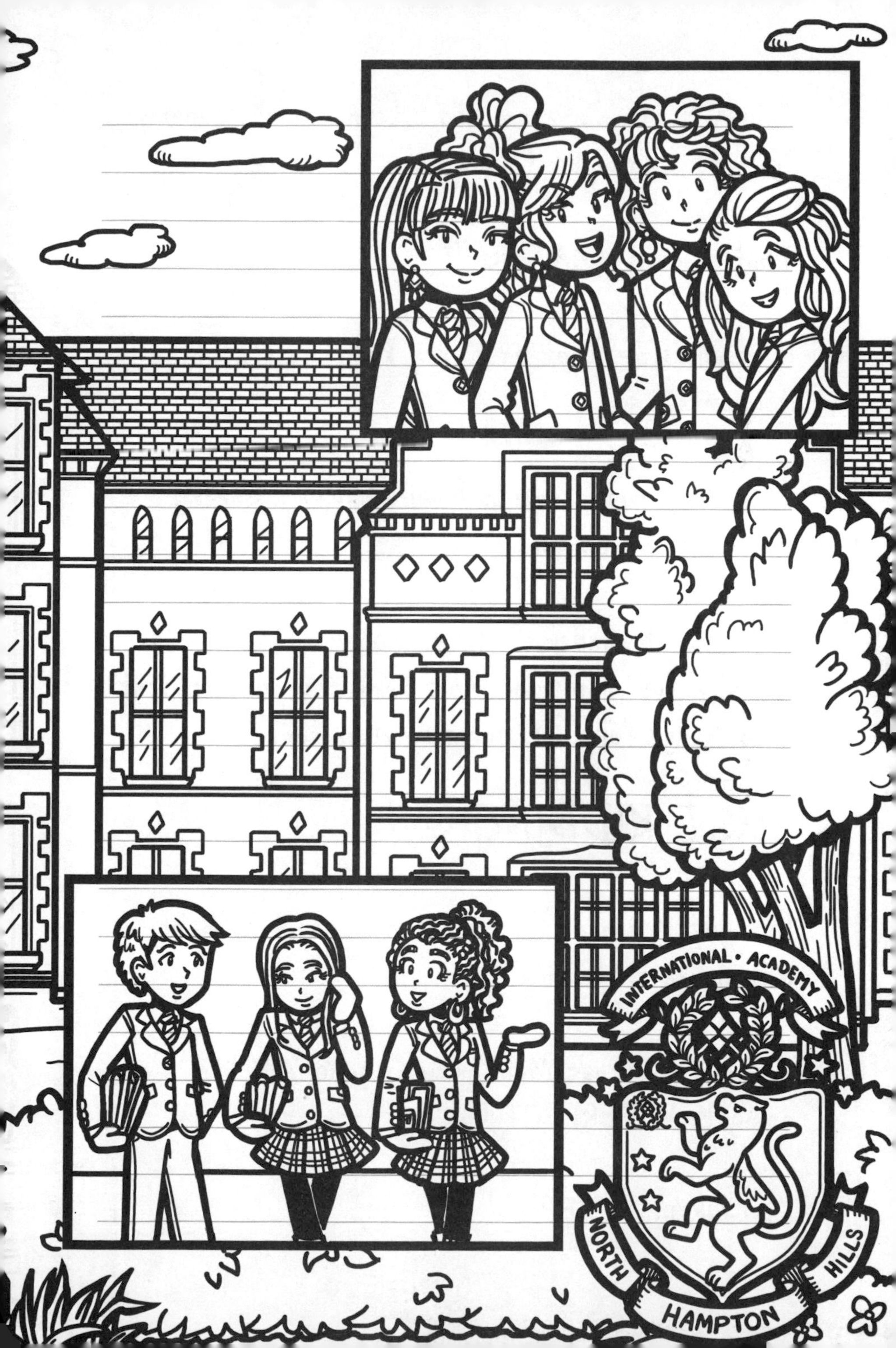
INTERNATIONAL · ACADEMY
NORTH
HAMPTON
HILLS

Calling North Hampton Hills International Academy "POSH" is an understatement!

That place is AMAZING!!!

It reminds me a lot of Harry Potter's school, Hogwarts.

I just hope MacKenzie is finally happy (assuming she actually even goes there).

Hmm . . . . I wonder if North Hampton Hills would award a full scholarship to a very deserving student in exchange for BUG extermination services?

JUST KIDDING ☺!!

But hey, it wouldn't be the first school to make a deal like that. RIGHT?!

Anyway, now that MacKenzie is gone, MY life is going to be PERFECT ☺!

And DRAMA FREE ☺!

Well, I need to stop ~~ranting~~ writing and get going.

I'm supposed to meet Chloe, Zoey, and Brandon at the CupCakery in twenty minutes, and I STILL need to change into my favorite dress.

The cupcakes there are to DIE for!!

SQUEEEEEEEE!

☺!!

It was really fun chillaxing with Chloe, Zoey, and Brandon at the CupCakery.

But inside my head I was doing my Snoopy "happy dance" while gleefully counting the number of MINUTES MacKenzie has been OUT of my life! . . .

12,584, 12,585, 12,586, 12,587, 12,588, 12,589 . . . !!

I'M . . . SO . . . HAPPY!!

ME, DOING MY SNOOPY "HAPPY DANCE"!!

The fact that MacKenzie was ACTUALLY gone was FINALLY starting to sink in.

I felt really HOPEFUL and like I had a whole NEW future ahead of me.

I was so distracted that at first I didn't notice Brandon staring at me.

Then he blushed and handed me the most beautiful cupcake with a pink heart on it.

"Nikki, I'm glad we're hanging out again. I know you've been through a lot lately, but I hope everything is okay," he said shyly as he brushed his shaggy bangs out of his eyes.

"Brandon, everything is just PERFECT!!" I gushed.

Then we just stared at each other and blushed.

All this staring, gushing, and blushing went on, like, FOREVER!! . . .

BRANDON AND ME, STARING, GUSHING,
AND BLUSHING AS WE SHARE A CUPCAKE!

OMG, it was SO romantic!

Suddenly dozens of butterflies started fluttering in my stomach.

It made me feel very giggly and a little queasy. All at the same time. Like I wanted to . . . vomit . . . rainbow-colored . . . CUPCAKE SPRINKLES!

SQUEEEEEEEEEEE ☺!!

As we stared into each other's eyes, I could definitely sense something KA-RAY-ZEE was about to happen.

AGAIN! Like, um . . . YOU KNOW ☺!!

Chloe and Zoey left from the table near ours to go to the shop next door to get strawberry smoothies. Which meant Brandon and I were alone ☺!

Mere words CANNOT begin to describe what happened next. . . .

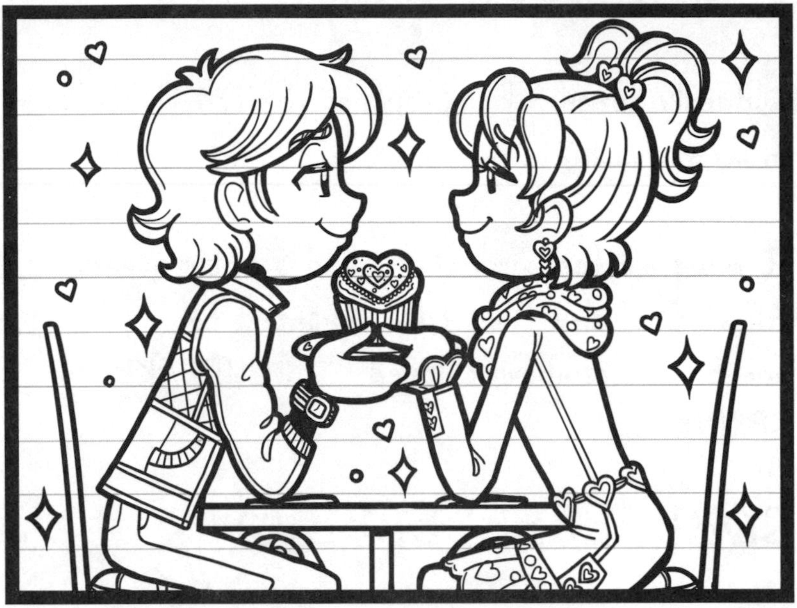

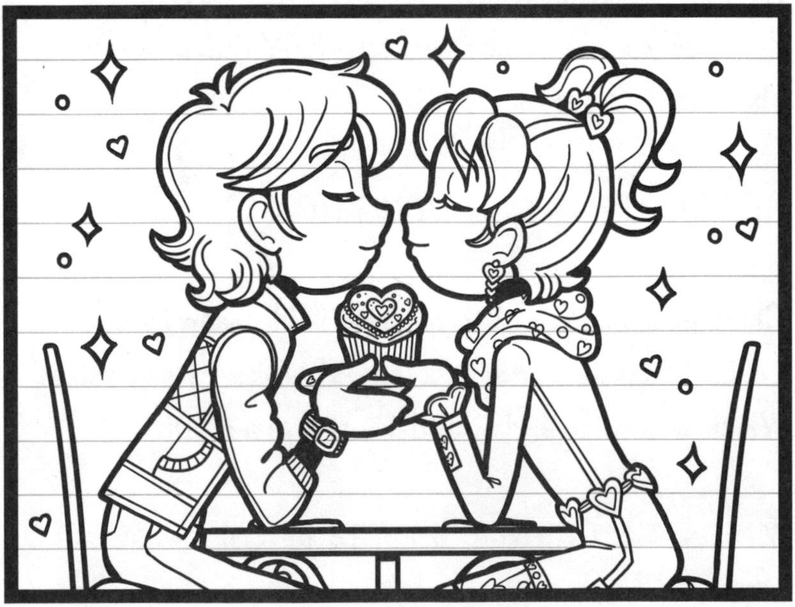

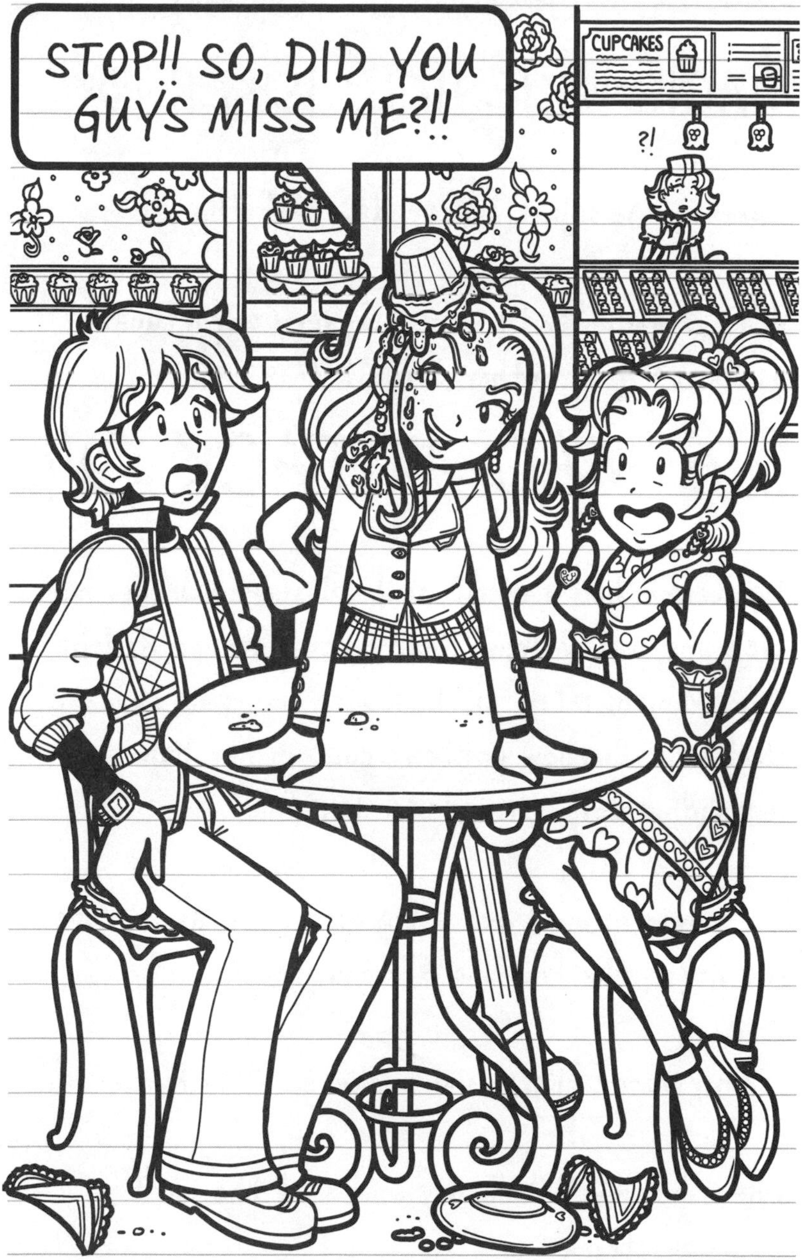
STOP!! SO, DID YOU GUYS MISS ME?!!
CUPCAKES
?!

OMG!! I could NOT believe it was actually . . .

MACKENZIE HOLLISTER ☹?!!

Somehow she'd just appeared out of thin air.

YEP! Brandon and I were the very unfortunate victims of yet another SNEAKY . . .

BIG MAC ATTACK ☹!!

MacKenzie had a HUGE smile plastered across her face and was wearing Ready for Revenge Red lip gloss. Which, BTW, clashed with our pink cupcake that had somehow gotten stuck in her hair and was sliding down the side of her face.

She slowly scraped off a big glob of smashed cupcake and licked the frosting off her finger.

"Sorry about that!" she snickered. "My BAD!"

Then she smiled wickedly and said the most ridiculous thing. . . .

MACKENZIE, RETURNING OUR CUPCAKE!

OMG! That cupcake fiasco was so disgusting,
I felt like throwing up AGAIN ☹!

That's when I suddenly realized I was completely
WRONG about MacKenzie. She WASN'T gone from
my life forever!! YET!! But I was about to "fix"
that little problem.

HOW?! By grabbing her wretched little neck and
force-feeding her cupcakes until frosting oozed
out of her ears.

MacKenzie was CRUEL and RUTHLESS! Not only
did she RUIN my cupcake dessert, but she rudely
INTERRUPTED my almost SECOND KISS with
Brandon ☹!

(Which, unlike the first kiss, did NOT involve helping
the needy children of the world!)

I looked right into her beady little eyes and could
see she'd done all that just to undermine my
relationship with Brandon.

"MacKenzie!!!" I gasped in shock. "WHAT are you doing here?!"

"I just came over to say hi. We haven't seen each other in AGES! And wow! You haven't changed a bit, Nikki!"

"That's probably because it's only been a week, one day, eight hours, fifty-four minutes, and thirty-nine seconds. But hey, who's counting?!" I muttered.

Then I totally lost it and screamed, "MacKenzie, next time try staying away LONG enough for me to actually start MISSING you! You know, like maybe twenty-seven YEARS!!" But I just said it inside my head, so no one else heard it but me.

I could not believe what that girl did next!

She totally ignored ME and started FLIRTING shamelessly with BRANDON!!

"So, Brandon, wanna hang out this weekend?
I'll tell you about North Hampton Hills. You'd love
it there. You should transfer!" she said, batting
her eyelashes all flirtylike as she twirled her hair
around and around her finger in a blatant attempt
to hypnotize him to do her evil bidding. . . .

MACKENZIE, SHAMELESSLY
FLIRTING WITH BRANDON!!

"Actually, MacKenzie, Nikki told me everything! Sorry, but I DON'T hang out with SOCIOPATHS!" Brandon said, shooting her a dirty look.

"Well, YOU shouldn't believe everything your little friend tells you, Brandon!" MacKenzie snarled. "Especially when she hasn't been taking her MEDS!"

I could NOT believe that girl was talking TRASH about me right to my face like that. Especially in front of my CRUSH!!

Then MacKenzie scrunched up her nose at me like she smelled something REALLY bad.

"So, Nikki, would you like a Tic Tac breath mint? All that GARBAGE you've been SPEWING about me is making your breath STINK!"

"No, MacKenzie. Actually, YOU need to use that breath mint WAY more than I do! You've been talking so much TRASH and telling so many LIES that YOUR breath stinks worse than my mom's cabbage-and-bologna casserole rotting in a hot garbage bag in July!" I shot back.

That's when MacKenzie got all up in my face like an ortho retainer.

"Nikki, you're a worthless FAKE!! You shouldn't even be attending WCD. Thank goodness I don't go there anymore."

"Oh, really? Well, thank goodness you LEFT! And, MacKenzie, YOU'RE such a FAKE, Barbie is JEALOUS!! But what I don't understand is how you can be so mean and cruel to other people! Is it because you're so insecure? Sorry, but no one is perfect. Not even you, MacKenzie. So you can stop pretending to be."

For a split second she actually looked kind of stunned. I guess I must have hit a nerve or something.

Or maybe she was wondering how I knew she was obsessed with trying to be perfect.

"Unless your name is Google, you need to stop acting like you KNOW everything, Nikki! I'm WARNING you! If you go blabbing my personal business, you're going to regret it. I've read your diary, and I know ALL your little secrets. So DON'T mess with me, or you and your pathetic friends will be kicked out of WCD so fast it will make your head spin!"

"This is between you and me, MacKenzie! Just keep my friends out of it! Dragging innocent people into this is NOT fair!"

"Not FAIR? Really?! You know what THAT sounds like? NOT. MY. PROBLEM!"

I just stared at her in disbelief as she stared back at me with her cold, icy blue eyes. Our conversation was interrupted when several students walked into the cupcake shop.

And get this!! They were dressed in the EXACT same school uniform as MacKenzie!

When she saw them, her mouth dropped open and she looked like she had just seen a ghost or something!

Of course that immediately made me VERY suspicious.

MacKenzie has lied SO often about SO much for SO long, I was beginning to wonder if she really even attended North Hampton Hills.

FINALLY! I was about to find out the TRUTH!

☺!!

WEDNESDAY—5:10 P.M.
AT THE CUPCAKERY

OMG! MacKenzie was acting totally SCHIZOID!

Just two minutes ago, she was Miss Thang with a funky attitude, talking trash and all up in my face like NOSE HAIR.

But NOW she was a nervous wreck and more uncomfortable than a fat, slimy worm on a hot sidewalk.

And I was LOVING every minute of it.

She frantically wiped the frosting out of her hair and then said to Brandon and me, "Well, I really should be going now. I have a ton of homework to do. Later!"

But before MacKenzie could sneak away, her classmates spotted her and rushed over to talk.

She quickly plastered on a fake smile. . . .

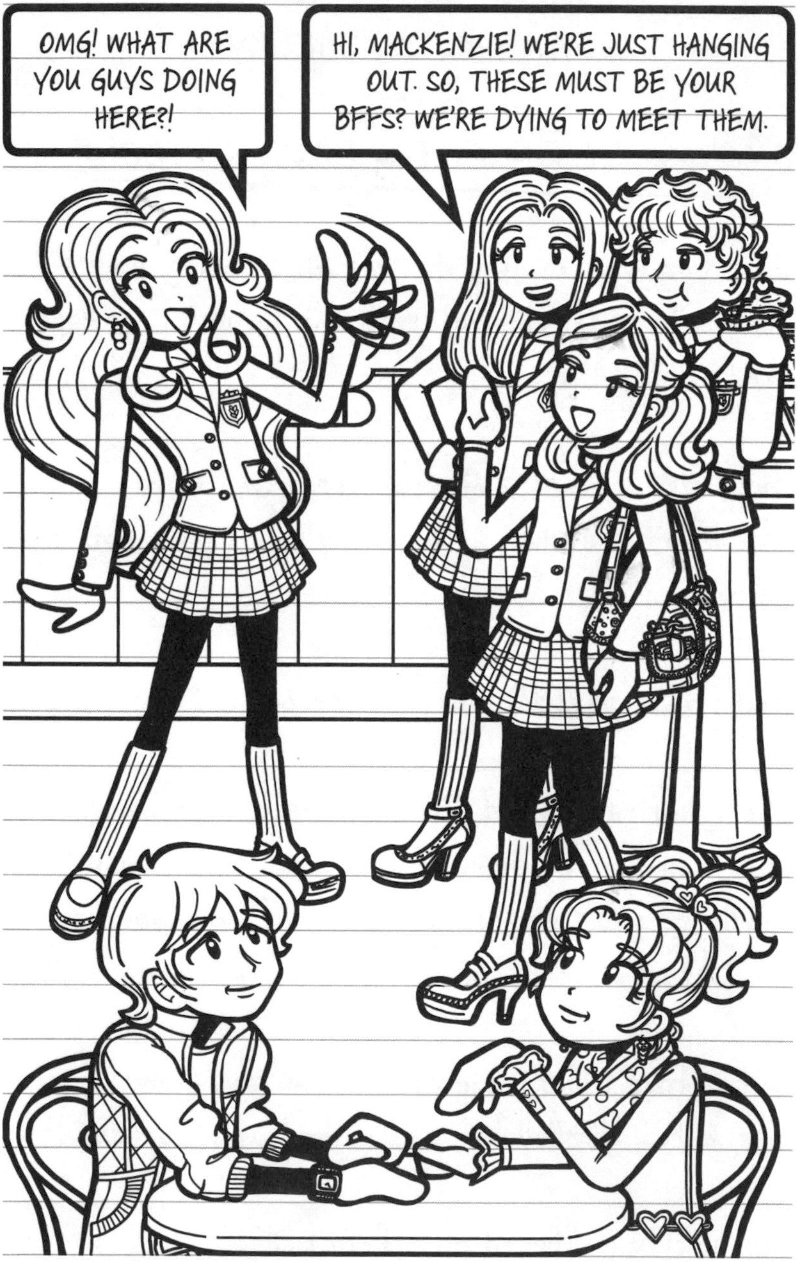
OMG! WHAT ARE YOU GUYS DOING HERE?!
HI, MACKENZIE! WE'RE JUST HANGING OUT. SO, THESE MUST BE YOUR BFFS? WE'RE DYING TO MEET THEM.

MacKenzie gazed nervously at Brandon and me. "Actually, they were just leaving. They both have a ton of homework to do. So maybe next time, okay?"

But in spite of her objections, her classmates hurried over to introduce themselves.

"Okay! So YOU must be Nikki! I'm Presli. OMG! MacKenzie told us all about her very cool band, Actually, I'm Not Really Sure Yet, and her record deal. It was SO nice of you to agree to stand in for her as lead singer while she had her tonsils removed. Anyway, we want Actually, I'm Not Really Sure Yet to perform at our eighth-grade graduation party, and MacKenzie said she'd think about it and let us know!"

"Hi there! I'm Sol, and YOU'RE Brandon, right?! You and MacKenzie are the CUTEST couple EVER! No wonder the two of you were crowned Sweetheart Prince and Princess at your Valentine's dance. MacKenzie said you'll probably be transferring to North Hampton Hills next year. You're going to LOVE it!"

"Hey, what's up, Nikki! I'm Evan, and I'm the editor of the school newspaper. MacKenzie told us you helped her with her SUPERpopular advice column, Miss Know-It-All. I'm trying to get her to do an advice column for our newspaper too."

"I know the two of you are really missing MacKenzie," Presli continued. "It was SO sweet of you to decorate her old locker! She showed us a photo, and it was ADORABLE!"

"Yeah! How many students would volunteer at Fuzzy Friends, run a book drive for the school library, ice-skate to earn money for charity, AND create a line of designer fashions for homeless animals?" Sol gushed. "MacKenzie's an ANGEL!"

That's when I totally lost it and screamed, "Wow! MacKenzie is just so WONDERFUL! I bet she farts GLITTER too!" But I just said it inside my head, so no one else heard it but me.

I was SO freaked out by all the stuff those kids were saying that I almost fell out of my chair.

32

It was like MacKenzie had STOLEN my identity or something.

I seriously considered calling the authorities and having her thrown in jail.

OMG!

Brandon and I were quietly FUMING!!

We were SO mad, our heads were about to EXPLODE!!

But the worst part was that MacKenzie just stood there with this stupid grin on her face, nodding like every word they were saying was TRUE.

Like, WHO does THAT?!!

It was clear to me why she'd tried to sneak off before they saw her.

It was going to get really complicated really fast with TWO Nikki Maxwells in the room.

I wanted to scream, "Will the REAL Nikki Maxwell PLEASE stand up!"

WHICH NIKKI IS THE REAL ME?!!

Completely fed up, Brandon glanced at the door and cleared his throat.

"Listen, Nikki, it's getting late. I think we should get going. It was really nice meeting all of you."

"Yeah, same here. Hopefully, we'll see you all again soon," I said sweetly as I plastered a big smile across my face, "IF MacKenzie decides to let HER band, Actually, I'm Not Really Sure Yet, play at your graduation party!"

Then I glared at MacKenzie like she was a wad of gum stuck to the bottom of my shoe.

That's when she started to panic.

"Um, wait, guys! Please, don't leave yet. I need to . . . um, explain a few things, okay?"

"Actually, MacKenzie, I've already heard quite enough! North Hampton Hills sounds like a really great school. I'm really, um . . . happy for you," I said.

MacKenzie blinked in surprise. "You are? Really? Thanks! Well, um . . . the least I can do is get you guys another cupcake. You never finished eating the last one."

"Thanks for the offer, MacKenzie. But don't worry about it," I said.

"Are you sure? I hear the double chocolate ones are really good. But my favorite is the red velvet with cream cheese frosting. Or I could buy you BOTH!" MacKenzie rambled.

Brandon and I just shook our heads.

We'd had all we could take of MacKenzie's CRAY-CRAY antics.

All she needed to complete her very bizarre act was some CIRCUS music.

We quickly headed for the door as MacKenzie continued to recite the cupcake menu.

Then, out of nowhere, she suddenly shouted, "Okay, great! It was cool hanging out with you. I miss you, too! Love you guys!"

Okay, THAT was totally weird. What alternate reality was SHE living in?

Or was she just suffering from some obscure disease, like, um . . . early-onset . . . middle-grade . . . DEMENTIA?

Once we were outside, Chloe and Zoey met back up with us in front of the cupcake shop.

"Chloe and Zoey! You'll NEVER in a million years guess who we just saw inside!" I exclaimed.

That's when we heard a strange tapping sound.

The four of us gasped and stared at the huge window of the CupCakery in disbelief.

Finally, Chloe and Zoey uttered . . .

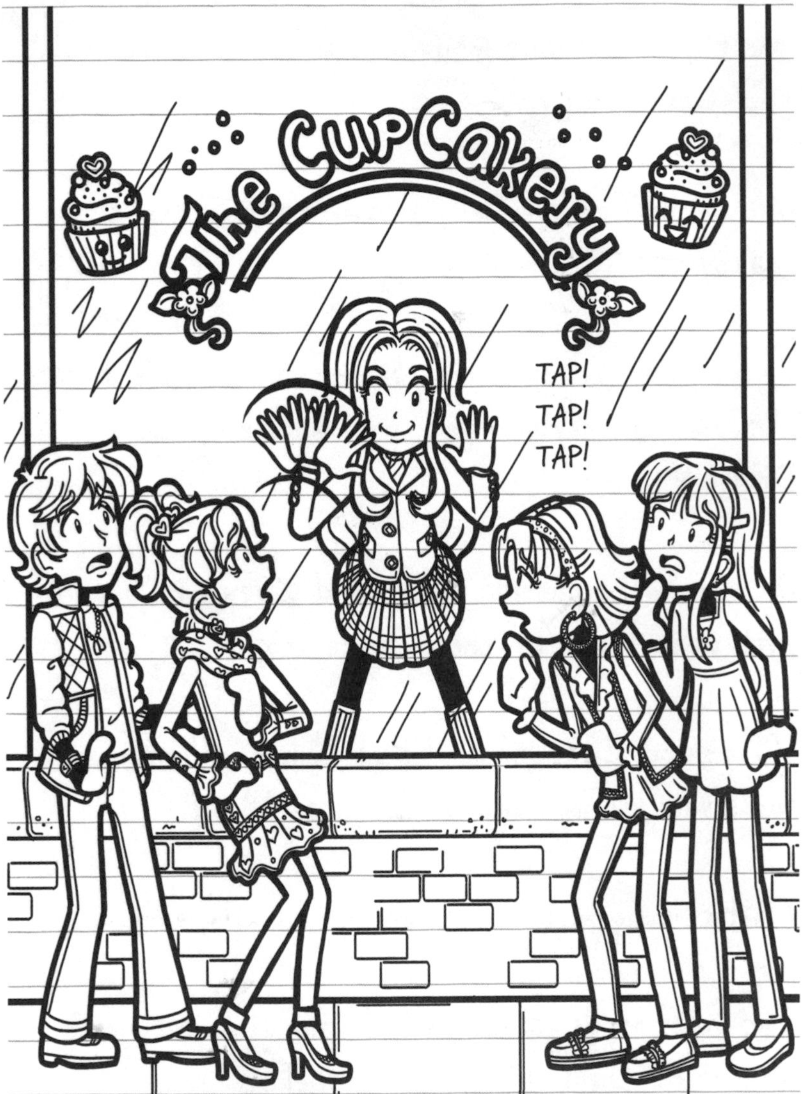
The CupCakery
TAP!
TAP!
TAP!

"UM, WAS IT . . . MACKENZIE?!!"

MacKenzie had pressed her face against the window and was frantically waving at us like we were leaving on a cruise ship or something.

Of course we all waved back at her.

Both of my BFFs stared at MacKenzie with perplexed looks on their faces.

"Is she sick or something?" Chloe wondered aloud.

"WHY is she acting so . . . strange? And . . . friendly?" Zoey pondered in awe.

"Listen, guys! Just keep smiling at her and slowly back away. I'll call you later tonight and fill you in," I explained.

Brandon and I said good-bye to Chloe and Zoey and then headed across the street to Fuzzy Friends.

We planned to hang out there for a half hour until my mom picked me up.

Although I hadn't been to Fuzzy Friends in a few weeks, it seemed more like months.

Once on the sidewalk, Brandon glanced warily over his shoulder at the cupcake shop.

"You know something? MacKenzie reminds me a lot of the stomach flu! Just when I think she's gone for good, she comes roaring back with a vengeance!"

"Tell me about it!" I sighed.

It was quite obvious that MacKenzie was up to something. I shuddered at the thought that we were possibly pawns in some scheme of hers.

I couldn't help but wonder whether that illness Brandon had mentioned was CONTAGIOUS.

Because I had a sinking feeling I was about to contract a really UGLY case of the MACKENZIE FLU too!

☹!!

As we walked along, Brandon and I agreed that MacKenzie was always creating DRAMA just to undermine our friendship. Which, BTW, included that nasty rumor that he had kissed me on a bet just to get a free pizza. Of course, I was DYING to ask him about it.

"So, um, did you actually win a FREE . . . pizza?"

"Oh, that?" He rolled his eyes in embarrassment. "Mr. Zimmerman said a camera company donated pizza gift cards to our photography team. So it had nothing whatsoever to do with . . . um, you know." He blushed. "You didn't believe that silly rumor, did you?"

"Of course not! I'm not THAT stupid. I knew all along that MacKenzie was lying! So I didn't believe that rumor for one second," I lied.

As we walked up the sidewalk to Fuzzy Friends, I immediately noticed something strange. . . .

BRANDON AND ME, DISCOVERING
AN ABANDONED DOG!

It was a beautiful, adorable, well-groomed golden retriever.

The dog curiously cocked its head and stared at us. As we approached, it stood up, wagged its tail, and seemed to be really friendly.

"Poor thing," I said. "I wonder who left it out here? And why?"

"I'm not sure. But it doesn't look like one of our dogs."

Brandon stooped over to pat its head and checked for an ID on its collar.

The dog licked his hand and then barked as if to say hello.

That's when we noticed the note attached to its collar.

I opened it and read it aloud. . . .

Dear Fuzzy Friends,

Unfortunately, I had to move into
a senior citizen building, and no
pets are allowed.

I love Holly very much, so please
take good care of her and her
critters! I know you will find
her a wonderful home.

Thank you for your kindness!

"Critters? What critters?" I asked, confused.

"Hmm. This box says 'For Holly.' So maybe her
toys and stuff are inside. Let's take a look,"
Brandon said.

Curious, we both peered inside the box. . . .

WE WERE VERY SHOCKED AND
SURPRISED BY WHAT WE FOUND!!

Lots of cute, sweet, wiggly little PUPPIES! We had a hard time counting them as they jumped, tumbled, and scampered inside the box.

But there seemed to be SEVEN in all! And, they were TOTALLY ADORABLE!! . . .

"I still have time before my mom gets here. Would you like me to help you take them inside and register them?" I asked.

"Yeah, thanks. But, to be honest, I'd rather we skip all the, um . . . . paperwork."

"Then HOW will people know Holly and her puppies are available for adoption?"

"That's exactly my point! Right now I don't want ANYONE to know Fuzzy Friends has eight more homeless animals, okay?"

"But WHY?! I don't understand!"

Brandon closed his eyes and sighed. "This is serious stuff, Nikki. Are you SURE you wanna know? I'm warning you! If I tell you, I might have to KILL you!" he teased half seriously.

"OMG! Brandon, is something wrong?"

"Well, according to our case manager, Fuzzy Friends

has been at full capacity all week. And it gets worse. We won't have room until Sunday morning! He has actually been refusing new animals," Brandon explained as a look of sheer frustration crept onto his face.

"Well, we can just get some extra cages and find some space. How about the storage room?"

"Nikki, it's not that simple. Based on the size of our center, we can only have a certain number of animals on the premises because of the city ordinances."

"Oh! I didn't know that."

"I absolutely HATE when this happens, because we're turning away animals, and not all places in the city have a no-kill policy like we do. So do you know what that means?" He paused and shook his head sadly.

It took a few seconds for me to figure it out. And then my heart sank!

"OH NO!" I groaned. "If Fuzzy Friends doesn't have room, that means Holly and her pups can't stay here! But what if they end up at . . ."

I gasped at the HORROR of it all. I could barely bring myself to say the words.

". . . one of th—those OTHER p-places?!" I stammered. "Brandon, we CAN'T let that happen!! What can we do?!"

"Well, I guess we can keep them here as long as no one knows about it. Including our case manager. It's a serious violation that could get us shut down, so I understand his concern. But I can't put Holly and her pups at risk like that either. I'd NEVER, EVER forgive myself if . . ." His voice cracked and trailed off as he gave Holly a big hug and buried his face in her fur.

She looked at Brandon sadly and whimpered.

Then she licked his face like he was a human lollipop until finally he broke into a big smile. . . .

50

BRANDON, THE HUMAN LOLLIPOP ☺!!

It was almost like she knew the serious situation she and her pups were in but didn't want Brandon to be upset about it.

Brandon's eyes started to glisten and fill with tears. He blinked and quickly wiped them away.

"Brandon, are you . . . okay?!"

"Um, I just had some dust in my eyes or something. I'm . . . fine," he muttered.

He was obviously LYING! The poor guy looked like his heart had been ripped right out of his chest. I got a huge lump in my throat and felt like crying too.

I felt just horrible for my friend and the eight abandoned dogs he'd already fallen in love with. Suddenly I had a huge surge of energy! Sorry, but I was NOT giving up without a FIGHT! "Listen, Brandon! I've got your back on this! Just tell me what I need to do!"

Brandon cocked his head and stared at me in disbelief. "Nikki, are you SERIOUS?!"

"As SERIOUS as a HEART ATTACK, dude!"

He grinned from ear to ear. "Yeah, me too! I guess I can ALWAYS count on you, Nikki!"

Then we gave each other a high five to seal our deal to keep Holly and her puppies safe until we could find good homes for them.

"So, I hope you're good at keeping secrets," Brandon said with a crooked smile.

Suddenly it became apparent that the task ahead of us was going to be far more difficult than Brandon and I had EVER imagined. . . .

"OMG! DID YOU JUST SAY 'SECRETS'?!" a voice squealed in excitement behind us.

Startled, Brandon and I nearly jumped out of our skins. I could NOT believe someone had been eavesdropping on our very personal and private conversation. We CRINGED and slowly turned around. I was PRAYING that it WASN'T who I thought!!

But, unfortunately, it WAS!! . . .

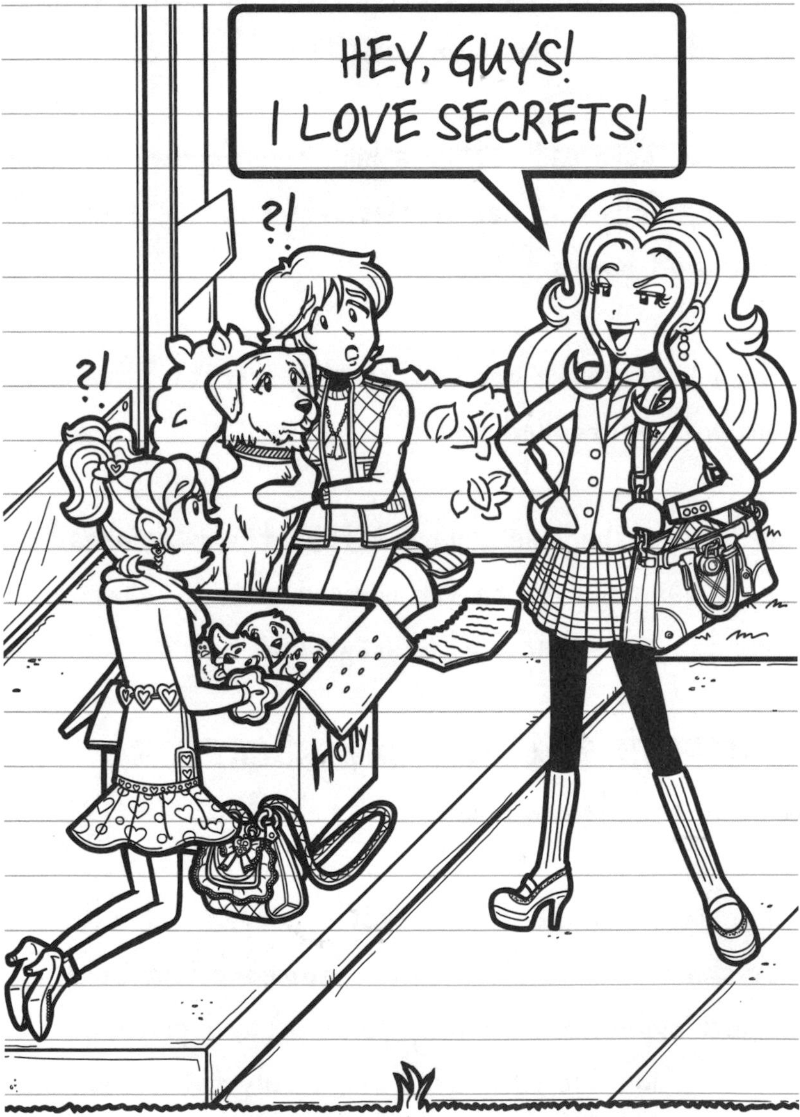
HEY, GUYS!
I LOVE SECRETS!
?!
?!
Holly

MACKENZIE! AGAIN ☹?!

It was the second BIG MAC ATTACK that day!

I suddenly got the very creepy feeling that she was STALKING us or something!

"So, what's the BIG SECRET?!! You can trust me. I won't tell a soul, I promise! You guys aren't in any kind of TROUBLE, are you?" she asked, staring at us suspiciously.

Brandon and I exchanged worried looks and then gazed nervously at MacKenzie.

It was quite obvious we were both thinking the EXACT same thing. . . .

OH, CRUD!!
☹!!!

"MacKenzie, WHAT are YOU doing here?!" I blurted out for the SECOND time today.

"Listen, Nikki, it wasn't MY fault those IDIOTS from my school got their facts about us all mixed up! But that little accident WAS my fault, so I wanted to personally deliver this," she said, opening her designer bag and taking out a cupcake box. I couldn't believe my eyes! Was MacKenzie actually doing something NICE for a change?

"So the ONLY reason you're here is to deliver a cupcake?" Brandon asked skeptically.

"Come on! Don't be ridiculous! You think I came here just to SPY on you? PUH-LEEZE! I have way more IMPORTANT things I could be doing, like dusting my FABULOUS shoe collection."

"Okay, let me get this straight. YOU bought US another cupcake?" I asked, raising an eyebrow.

56

MacKenzie shook her head and giggled sarcastically. . . .

UM, I DIDN'T EXACTLY BUY YOU A NEW CUPCAKE. BUT ALL YOU HAVE TO DO IS PICK OUT THE LINT AND A FEW STRAY HAIRS, AND YOUR OLD CUPCAKE WILL BE AS GOOD AS NEW! YUM, YUM!!

"OMG! MacKenzie, you SHOULDN'T have!!" I muttered.

I didn't know which was more DISGUSTING. That nasty-looking cupcake or the fact that I had just thrown up inside my mouth.

"You don't have to thank me!" MacKenzie smiled.

"No, I meant it. You really should NOT have done this! ICK! WHAT is that green gooey stuff?" I asked.

"Who knows!" MacKenzie shrugged. "The waitress at the CupCakery cleared your table and tossed it. But I fished it out of the garbage and brought it here because I wanted you two little LOVEBIRDS to have it!"

EWW! That's when I threw up in my mouth again.

Brandon and I just rolled our eyes. It was quite obvious that MacKenzie had something up her sleeve and was just playing mind games with us.

"What's wrong? You two don't look very happy," she scoffed.

"Why would we be?" I shot back. "You've been practically STALKING us!"

"Well, Miss Smarty-Pants, maybe I wanted to take the scenic route home today!"

I narrowed my eyes at her. "MacKenzie, you WERE spying on us! Just admit it!!"

"Shut up, Nikki! I've got a perfectly good explanation! I was just, um . . ." She hesitated.

I had to admit, MacKenzie looked silly standing there thinking and making weird faces like she was suffering from severe constipation.

I rolled my eyes. "Well, we're WAITING! . . ."

"Actually . . . I was, um. Okay, FINE!" She placed her hands on her hips and glared at us. "So what if I was SNOOPING?! Stop pretending you're so

PERFECT! You dirty, LAW-BREAKING, animal shelter . . . um, RULE VIOLATORS! These mangy mutts, er, I mean . . . POOR DOGS are in extreme . . . DANGER! Thank goodness I got here in time to . . . SAVE THEM!"

Brandon and I froze and gasped. . . .

"So you DID hear us!" I said, trying not to panic.

"Every. Shady. Sneaky. DETAIL! I just hope your little secret doesn't get leaked to the Channel 6 investigative news team," MacKenzie snarled. "Then Fuzzy Friends will lose its license and be shut down! And every last one of these flea-infested MUTTS will be out on the street. Probably getting RUN OVER! Or worse! All because YOU two refused to follow the rules!"

Brandon looked like MacKenzie had just slapped him. He stared down at his feet.

Her harsh words and accusations had obviously knocked the wind (and good intentions) right out of him.

"Brandon, I expected so much BETTER from YOU! I thought you had integrity!" MacKenzie scolded him as he hung his head in shame.

"WHAT is wrong with you, MacKenzie?!" I cried angrily. "You transferred to your dream school and have everything you've ever wanted. Why do you STILL have to DESTROY anything that breathes?"

"Oh, I dunno!" She smirked as she took out her cell phone. "I guess bad habits are hard to break!"

Desperate, I tried to reason with her.

"MacKenzie, can't you see the lives of these innocent animals are at stake?! Not every shelter in this city is safe!" I explained, blinking back tears.

Holly must have sensed I was upset or something because she suddenly bared her teeth, growled, and lunged at MacKenzie.

Brandon grabbed her collar just in time. "Whoa, girl! Calm down! Everything's fine!"

Alarmed, MacKenzie cautiously backed away from Holly. "That dog just tried to ATTACK ME! Keep that thing away from me or I'll call animal control! That savage beast is . . . DANGEROUS!"

OMG! I was SO angry, I wanted to slap that girl into tomorrow. . . .

"You say that like it's a BAD thing!" She sneered as she dialed a number on her cell phone.

Then MacKenzie did the unthinkable.

It was like she had stooped to a new LOW and started DIGGING.

"Hello? Is this the Channel 6 news tip hotline? I just found out some dirt on a local animal shelter. I think they're ABUSING animals! Yes, I'll hold."

Brandon looked overwhelmed and totally defeated.

He just sat on the step, staring like a zombie and quietly petting Holly.

Thanks to MacKenzie, Brandon stood to lose TWO things that he CHERISHED . . .

Fuzzy Friends, and Holly and her pups.

His lofty DREAM of helping animals and keeping them safe was quickly turning into his

WORST NIGHTMARE.

And there wasn't a thing we could do about it!!

!!

WEDNESDAY—5:48 P.M.
AT FUZZY FRIENDS

Calling this FIASCO a nightmare was an understatement ☹!!

MacKenzie was patiently waiting on hold to report Fuzzy Friends in hopes of closing it down.

I had to do SOMETHING! But what?!

I finally came up with four ideas. Unfortunately, each of them had a DOWNSIDE. . . .

1. THE FUNKY PHONE: I could grab MacKenzie's cell phone and quickly toss it into the sewer drain near the curb. Then she wouldn't have a phone to be able to report us.

But I could end up in JAIL for destruction of property. And, even worse, to REPLACE her expensive designer phone, I'd probably have to pay her my weekly allowance for thirteen years, nine months, and two weeks ☹!

2. THE DIVA DASH: Apparently, Holly doesn't like MacKenzie! I could interrupt her phone call AND exercise Holly, by allowing the dog to chase a screaming and hysterical MacKenzie all the way home.

But that would probably be CRUELTY to an ANIMAL! And a little cruel to Holly, too!

3. THE SMUSHED CUPCAKE CAPER: I could take that disgusting cupcake and shove it down MacKenzie's throat. Then she WOULDN'T be able to TALK about Fuzzy Friends (or anything else, for that matter).

But that could be MESSY! And possibly require a trip to the emergency room for doctors to surgically remove both the cupcake and my arm from her throat.

4. THE JUST CLOWNING AROUND: I could convince Brandon to run away with me and the dogs and join the circus. Then we'd spend the rest of our lives performing a funny clown act in SUPERcute costumes. . . .

BRANDON, THE DOGS, AND I
RUN AWAY AND JOIN THE CIRCUS!!

But then we'd miss our family and friends. I've also heard they get VERY SMELLY on hot summer days!

"They" meaning the CIRCUSES, not our family and friends.

After careful consideration, it appeared that the Smushed Cupcake Caper was probably the BEST idea overall.

NOT ☹!!

This situation was HOPELESS!

My mom was going to be picking me up any minute now, and I'd have to say good-bye to Holly and her pups FOREVER!

I sighed sadly and blinked back tears.

I was seriously reconsidering the Cupcake Caper when I came up with a wickedly CUNNING new idea!

Yes, it was a long shot, but it was our only hope!

"Well, Brandon, thanks to MacKenzie, it looks like Fuzzy Friends is going to be closed down soon," I said loud enough for MacKenzie to hear.

MacKenzie, who was STILL on hold, gave me a very smug look.

OMG! I wanted so badly to WIPE that little SMIRK right off her face, but instead I continued.

"Anyway, after dealing with all this drama, I've worked up a really big appetite. So I think I'm going to head back over to the CupCakery to try a few of those awesome cupcakes that MacKenzie recommended."

Of course Brandon looked at me like I was insane.

"Nikki! HOW can you be thinking about CUPCAKES at a time like this?!" he exclaimed.

"Um, because I'm HUNGRY? Anyway, while I'm there, I'm going to hang out with MacKenzie's new friends from North Hampton Hills. They seemed SO friendly. And I'm really looking forward to hearing even more of the fantastic LIES that MacKenzie has told them. But SOMEBODY needs to keep it real and tell them the TRUTH!! Wanna come, Brandon? It should be FUN!"

He finally caught on and gave me a sly grin.

"Sure, Nikki! But let's take the dogs inside first. Now that I think about it, I'd practically KILL for a Sweet Revenge Devil's Food cupcake!"

MacKenzie lowered her phone and nervously EYEBALLED us, all evil-like.

"Don't you DARE talk TRASH about me to my new friends. Better yet, I'M coming with you!!"

"No! You need to STAY right here and save the lives of these POOR dogs!" I said sarcastically.

"Do you think I care about these mangy mutts?!"

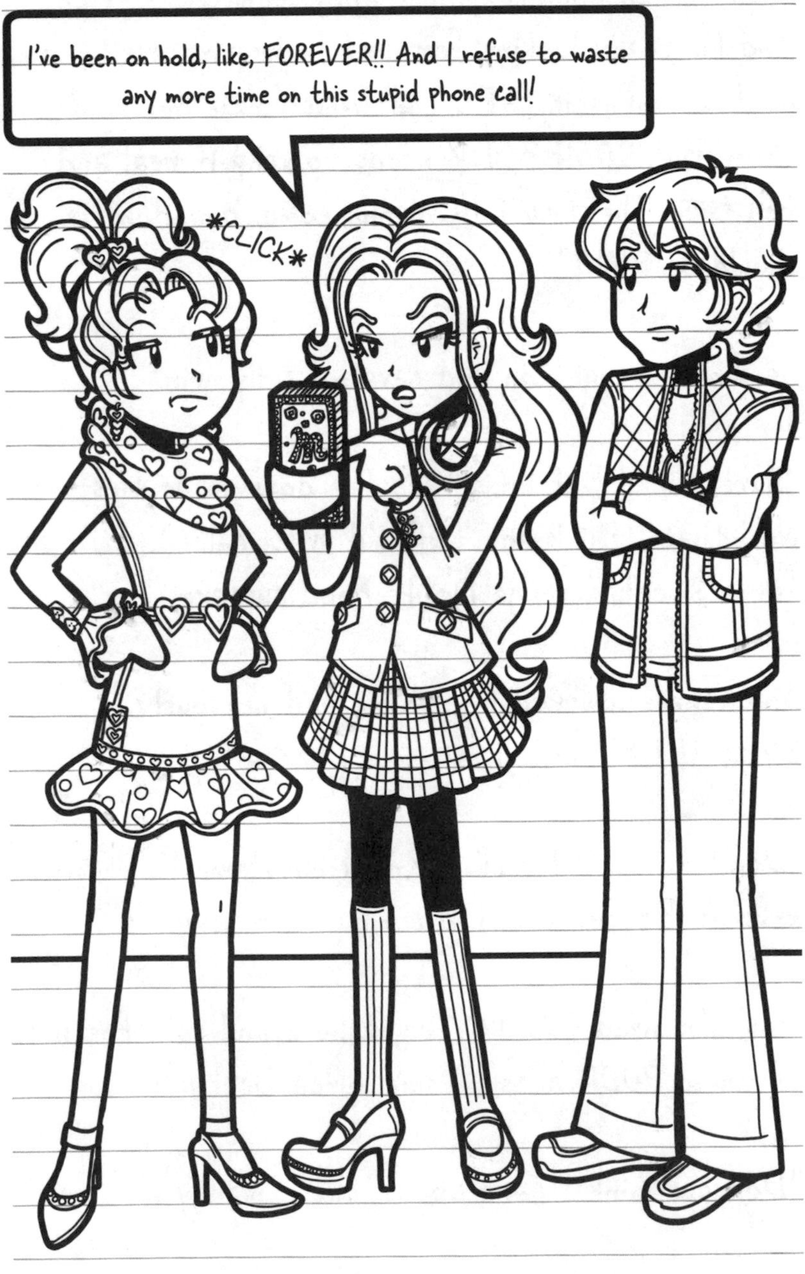
I've been on hold, like, FOREVER!! And I refuse to waste any more time on this stupid phone call!
CLICK

MacKenzie angrily ended her phone call and stuffed her cell phone back into her purse.

Then she narrowed her eyes and scowled at Brandon and me. "Listen! You two better stay away from my friends or I'll make sure you never see these little flea-infested furballs again."

"Oh, really?! Is that a THREAT?" I scoffed.

"NO! It's a PROMISE!!" she snarled.

Then she turned and sashayed back across the street to the CupCakery.

I just HATE it when that girl sashays!!

As Brandon and I watched her leave, we sighed in relief.

Thank goodness the dogs were safe!

For the moment, anyway.

Brandon brushed his shaggy bangs out of his eyes and just stared at me for what seemed like FOREVER.

"WHAT?!!" I asked defensively.

Slowly a smile spread across his face until it was ear to ear.

"How did you shut MacKenzie down like that?!" he asked. "I'd pretty much given up hope. I REALLY appreciate what you did just now."

I looked into his big brown eyes and could see he sincerely meant it.

A wave of emotion washed over me, and I got a big lump in my throat. But more than anything, I felt really good that I had Brandon's back and was there for him when he needed me.

Then I shrugged nervously and started babbling like I had totally lost my mind. "Thanks, Brandon!

But YOU'RE a lifesaver! And after we find these dogs a home, you'll be a HERO! You're also a nice person, a good friend, and . . . um, I bet you fart glitter too!"

YES! I actually said THAT to Brandon!!

Somehow it just kind of slipped out of my mouth. I was SO embarrassed.

Brandon and I had a really big laugh at my silly little joke!

"Come on, Nikki! Let's get these dogs inside. I bet they're starving," Brandon said happily as he picked up the box of puppies.

And he was right! Holly gobbled her food and then patiently nursed her hungry puppies.

Then the pups played in their bowl of puppy chow like it was one of those plastic ball pits for toddlers. . . .

BRANDON AND ME, FEEDING
HOLLY AND HER PUPS!

Although we had successfully averted a near disaster, Brandon and I STILL needed to come up with a plan.

We had no idea when the dreaded MACKENZIE FLU was going to STRIKE again!

And, unfortunately, there was no VACCINE!!

MacKenzie is a scheming, conniving SNAKE, so I knew it would be way too risky to keep the dogs at Fuzzy Friends for the rest of the week.

That's when I came up with yet another
BRILLIANT idea.

"Listen, Brandon! Why don't we simply take turns
taking care of the dogs at our HOMES until Fuzzy
Friends has space on Sunday?"

"I don't know, Nikki. Just one dog is a HUGE
responsibility. Taking care of eight of them would
be EXHAUSTING!"

"Yeah, but it's ONE dog and seven little puppies.
And since the mother dog feeds them and stuff,
there's not that much we need to do. Come on,
Brandon!"

After thinking it over for a few minutes, he
finally agreed. "Okay, Nikki! I'll take the first day
since they're already here. But we'll need to find
more volunteers."

I knew MY mom would definitely say YES to ME
keeping the dogs for a day! Just a few weeks ago
she'd let my bratty little sister, Brianna, keep

Rover the fish (a classroom pet) at our house for an ENTIRE weekend!

"I'm sure I can keep the dogs for a day too!" I said excitedly. "So now we'll only need TWO more people!"

"Great!" Brandon smiled. "Why don't you talk to Chloe and Zoey, and I'll talk to the guys. I think this plan just might work!"

Anyway, I'm SUPERexcited because I've always wanted a dog! I'd love it and hug it and kiss it and squeeze it and NEVER, EVER let it GO!! SQUEEEEE ☺!!

And NOW I'm going to get the chance to take care of Holly and her seven teeny-weeny, cutie-patootie, snuggly-wuggly, adorable wittle puppies for an ENTIRE twenty-four hours!!!

Hey, how hard can it be?!

☺!!!
...

WEDNESDAY—8:10 P.M.
IN MY BEDROOM

Okay, there's GOOD NEWS and some BAD NEWS!
First the GOOD NEWS.

When I told Chloe and Zoey about how Brandon
and I had found Holly and her puppies abandoned
on the front step of Fuzzy Friends, they were
SUPERexcited to help out.

So this is our plan: Brandon will be keeping the dogs
tonight, I'll have them tomorrow night, Chloe will
have them Friday night, and Zoey will have them
Saturday night.

Then on Sunday morning we'll return the dogs
to Fuzzy Friends so they can be placed in
loving homes.

Since Theodore Swagmire's family owns the Queasy
Cheesy pizza chain, he volunteered a pizza delivery
van and driver to transport the dogs anywhere
we need to go.

Okay, now for the BAD NEWS ☹!!

Everything was going as planned until I ran into a BIG, FAT, MESSY, totally unexpected COMPLICATION ☹!

After dinner I was helping my mom put dishes into the dishwasher. It was the perfect time to casually mention the dog situation.

I told her that, due to a family emergency, a good friend of mine needed a pet sitter for his dog, Holly (well, it was kinda true).

Then I ~~asked~~ BEGGED her to PLEASE let me keep the dog overnight on Thursday.

Of course, I conveniently left out the part about the dog having seven rambunctious puppies. I didn't want Mom to FREAK OUT over that very minor little detail!

But after talking to her, it was ME who totally FREAKED OUT. . . .

ME AND MOM, HAVING A LITTLE CHAT!

Her LAME excuse about it being "bad timing" made no sense WHATSOEVER!!

What does it matter if the dog has a little accident on the carpet tomorrow or TWO MONTHS from now?!

Either way you just clean it up! DUH!!!

Sorry, Mom, but if you let Brianna keep a pet overnight, then WHY can't I?!!

It's NOT fair!

Especially since I'm OLDER, more MATURE, and ten times more RESPONSIBLE than Brianna.

Come on! She accidentally murdered poor Rover the fish by giving him a bubble bath, remember?!!

Like, WHO does that?!!

Mom, if YOU were an ANIMAL, which of these two people would you want to be YOUR pet sitter?! . . .

PLEASE SELECT
THE PERFECT PET SITTER!!

☐ BRIANNA,
PET SITTING
ROVER THE FISH

☐ ME,
PET SITTING
HOLLY
THE DOG

I thought so!! I rest my CASE!!

Mom, I don't WANT to keep Holly "maybe in a few months"!

I want to keep her NOW!!

Who knows?! I might be DEAD in a few months!!

And then you'll be at my funeral SOBBING YOUR EYES OUT and rambling hysterically about how you'll NEVER, EVER forgive yourself for NOT letting me keep a pet overnight, especially after you let Brianna do it and she's a lot younger than me.

So thank you, Mom, for completely RUINING my life, endangering eight innocent dogs, and giving me LOW SELF-ESTEEM, which will probably require YEARS of intensive therapy.

Because you obviously LOVE Brianna way more than you love me ☹!!

I need to text Brandon and tell him the very bad news that my mom won't let me keep the dogs.

He's going to be really disappointed. I feel horrible that I let him down like this.

But right now I'm just too upset.

I plan to spend the rest of the night just sitting on my bed in my pajamas, STARING at the wall, SULKING.

☹!!!...

AAAAAAAAAAAAAAAAHH!!!!!

(That was me screaming in FRUSTRATION!!)

I have a major project due tomorrow in biology. And it's an entire third of my grade. Things have been so KA-RAY-ZEE the past week that I'd COMPLETELY forgotten about it!

The LAST thing I wanted to do was to procrastinate and then just throw something together the night before, like I did for my *Moby Dick* book report back in December.

I'd made this silly video that starred Brianna as a whale that said "ROAR!!" So I was shocked and surprised when I got an A+ on it ☺!

I decided to finish my SULKING later because I needed to get started on my bio project. Only I didn't have the slightest idea what I was going to do.

Then my mom yelled, "Nikki! Don't forget to take the clothes out of the dryer, fold them up, and put them away BEFORE you go to bed!" . . .

ME, TAKING LAUNDRY OUT OF THE DRYER

The laundry included four pairs of my dad's long underwear that he wears to work on colder days.

They actually look a lot like those one-piece footie pajamas that toddlers wear.

I was about to fold up the last one of them when I suddenly got the most brilliant idea!

Since Dad still had three pairs left, I decided that he probably wouldn't mind if I borrowed one for my bio project.

Besides, he is always harping about how important it is for me to get good grades so I can get a scholarship to a major university. And his long underwear would technically be helping me get a good grade. RIGHT??

So I confiscated them, took out my paint and markers, opened my biology book, and got busy at the kitchen table! . . .

ME, DILIGENTLY WORKING ON
MY ~~DAD'S LONG UNDERWEAR~~
BIO PROJECT!

I finally finished my project a little before midnight,
and I think it came out pretty good.

Especially considering the fact THAT it was based on a wacky idea I had while folding laundry. I just hope my teacher gives me a passing grade on it.

Anyway, now that my bio project is out of the way, I can finish SULKING ☺!!

I can't believe the woman who gave birth to me let Brianna keep a pet overnight but is REFUSING to let ME do the EXACT SAME THING ☹!

Life is SO unfair!!

I guess I'll tell Brandon the bad news tomorrow.

I just hope we can find another person to take my place.

☹!!

I was seriously dreading having to tell Brandon I couldn't keep the dogs.

It didn't help matters that he was happily waiting for me at my locker. Then he went on and on about how great the dogs were doing!

When I finally got up the courage to break the news, I interrupted him and said, "Um, Brandon, there's something really important I need to tell you."

But he said, "Really? Because there's something really important I need to tell YOU!"

He started gushing about how thankful and lucky he was to have me as a friend!!

Which made it even MORE difficult for me to tell him.

Then he said, "So, I'll drop the dogs by your house right after school today, okay?"

But before I could answer and say, "Actually, Brandon, you CAN'T drop the dogs by my house!! That's what I've been trying to tell you for the past ten minutes," he said, "Later, Nikki! See you in bio!" and disappeared into the crowded hallway.

The whole thing was SO FRUSTRATING ☹!!!

So now I had to try to explain everything to him AGAIN when I saw him in bio.

Only right before bio, I went into the girls' bathroom and stood in front of the mirror and practiced telling Brandon the bad news.

But I practiced too long and ended up four minutes late for bio, which meant I completely missed the chance to tell him the bad news AGAIN!

I just KNEW my teacher was going to be SUPERirritated with me for handing my project in late, and maybe even take a few points off.

But the strangest thing happened. . . .

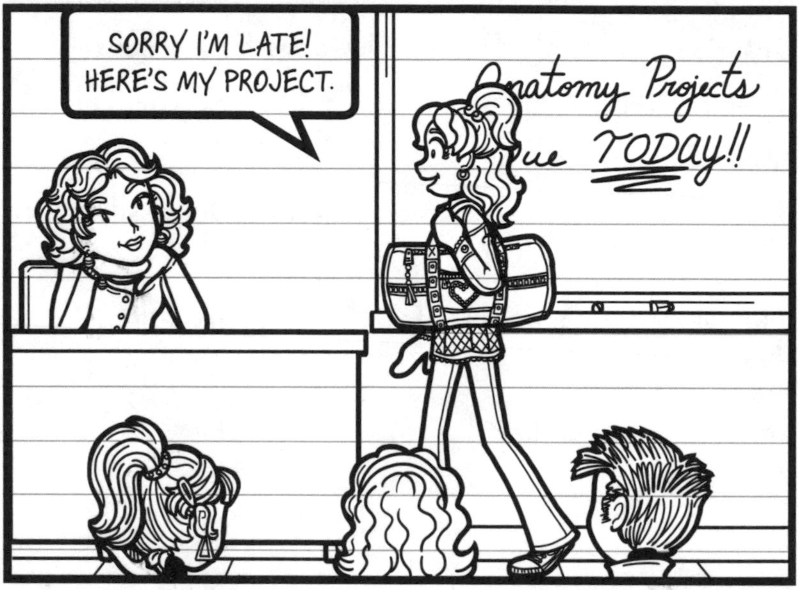
SORRY I'M LATE! HERE'S MY PROJECT.
Anatomy Projects Due TODAY!!

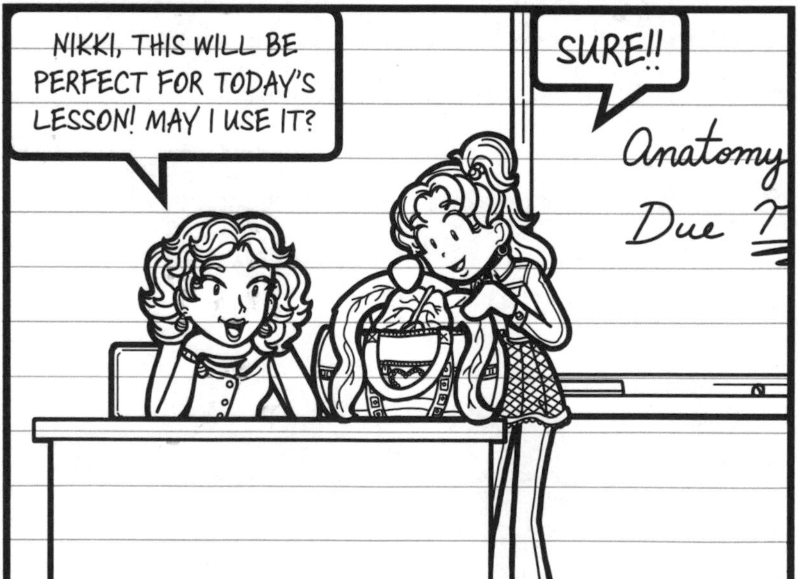
NIKKI, THIS WILL BE PERFECT FOR TODAY'S LESSON! MAY I USE IT?
SURE!!

My teacher actually LOVED my project!

She said it was not only creative, but very realistic.

As a matter of fact, she was SO impressed that she asked for a volunteer to WEAR it while she taught today's lesson on the human body.

Then she waited patiently for a student to raise his/her hand.

But I already knew she was wasting her time.

Who'd be STUPID enough to wear my dad's long underwear with the HUMAN ANATOMY painted on it in front of a classroom of their middle-school peers?!

Well, okay!

I'll rephrase the question. . . .

WHO, other than ME, would be that STUPID?! . . .

CLASS, THIS IS WHAT COMPLETE
HUMILIATION LOOKS LIKE!!

Most of the students must have thought the lesson was hilarious, because they snickered and giggled the entire time I was up there.

OMG! I was SO embarrassed.

I looked like some . . . FREAK who'd been in a really bad . . . parachuting accident and had somehow gotten . . . turned inside out.

Anyway, after class was over my teacher thanked me for creating such a wonderful project and sharing it with my classmates.

Then she suggested I enter it in the citywide science fair that our school would be hosting tomorrow after school.

Like, WHY would I want to HUMILIATE myself in front of the ENTIRE city?!

That's when I completely lost it and screamed, "I'm really SORRY, Ms. Kincaid! But I can't discuss the science fair right now. I need to rush outside, dig a really deep hole, crawl into it, and DIE!!"

Of course, I just said it inside my head, so no one else heard it but me.

Right now I'm hiding out in the girls' bathroom writing all this.

Unfortunately, I'll probably NEVER be able to do the laundry again. WHY?

Because I'm ALLERGIC to LONG UNDERWEAR!!

Anyway, I never got a chance to talk to Brandon.

So I've decided NOT to tell him!

Instead, I'm going to keep the dogs as planned.

I'll just HIDE them in my bedroom the entire time so that Mom and Dad will never even know they're in the house.

I'm sure the dogs will mostly just hang out in their cage and eat and sleep all day long.

And since the mother dog is there watching her puppies, that means LESS work for me!

Besides, I'll only be HIDING them in my room for twenty-four hours!

Hey, how hard can it be?!

☺!!

I thought the school day would NEVER end! I was
DYING to go home so I could get everything ready
for Holly and her puppies.

First I cleaned my room (the last thing I wanted
was for one of the dogs to nibble on that
ten-day-old moldy pizza slice under my bed).
Then I puppy-proofed it (my room, not the pizza).

And just in case Brianna decided to SNOOP around
once she got home from school, I cleared out enough
space in my closet to hide the dog cage.

When Brandon finally dropped off the dogs, I
excitedly took them upstairs to my bedroom.

OMG! They were so CUTE, I almost . . . melted
into a . . . puddle of . . . sweet, sticky . . . um, goo!

When Chloe and Zoey came over to visit, they
immediately fell in love with the dogs too. . . .

CHLOE AND ZOEY MEET THE DOGS!!

Holly and one sleepy puppy took a little nap, while the six other pups ran around my room, getting into all kinds of mischief.

The smallest puppy cuddled with Brianna's teddy bear, one chewed on a gym sock, while another played hide-and-seek under my bed.

They were SO cute ☺!!

I told Chloe and Zoey that my only worry was having to leave the dogs alone in my bedroom for extended periods, like during meals.

That's when Chloe said she had already thought about that problem and had come up with the PERFECT solution. She reached into her backpack and took out what looked like two old-fashioned cell phones.

Then she said . . .

CHLOE GIVES ME A BABY MONITOR SET
FOR THE DOGS!

Her mom had used it for Chloe's little brother when he was an infant.

Chloe explained that I was supposed to leave the speaker unit in my bedroom with the dogs and take the receiver part with me.

Then I'd be able to hear what the dogs were up to in my bedroom. Now, how COOL is THAT ☺?!! This baby monitor was a brilliant idea and would make taking care of the dogs A LOT easier.

"Until you decide to use them, I think we need to hide them somewhere," Chloe said, looking around the room. She grabbed my backpack off my chair and placed the baby monitor set inside. "Perfect!"

"Thanks, Chloe! Now, if I could only get rid of my parents for the entire evening! I'm afraid they might hear the dogs!"

That's when Zoey said she had already thought about that problem and had come up with the PERFECT solution.

She reached into her purse. "Here, Nikki! TWO MOVIE TICKETS!!" she exclaimed.

"Thanks, Zoey! But how am I supposed to take eight dogs to a MOVIE?!!" I asked, confused.

"They're NOT for YOU, silly! They're for your PARENTS! I bought tickets for the prequel of that new sci-fi blockbuster! It lasts three and a half hours! With the travel time there and back, your parents will be out of the house AND out of your hair for most of the night!"

I gave Chloe and Zoey a really big HUG! They're the BEST BFFs EVER!!

Thanks to them, I was going to be the PERFECT PET SITTER!!

☺!!

At first I was going to keep the dogs a secret from Brianna.

Mainly because she has a nasty habit of BLABBING any and everything to Mom and Dad.

But there was no way I was going to be able to hide eight dogs from Mom and Dad without a little help.

I didn't have a choice but to trust her.

Do you want to know the ONLY thing more exhausting than taking care of Brianna?

Taking care of SEVEN little Briannas with bigger ears and more hair on their backs.

So it was no surprise when they fell completely head over heels in love with each other at first sight. . . .

BRIANNA HUGS HOLLY AND HER PUPPIES!

I didn't realize how much she and the puppies had in common:

1. They're really loud and smell funny.

2. They're wiggly, messy, and like following me around the house.

3. They could use some additional potty training.

AND

4. They can get away with practically anything because they're SO ridiculously CUTE!!

They're like sisters and brothers from another mother!

However, the downside is that now Brianna is pestering me nonstop about "playing with the doggies."

I was in the kitchen doing my geometry homework when she walked in.

"Nikki! Can I let the doggies out of their cage and play with them for a little while? PLEASE! PLEASE! PLEASE! PLEASE! PLEASE!"

"Not until I finish my homework, Brianna. If you let them out of their cage, you have to keep a close eye on the puppies. Or else they'll get into trouble."

Brianna pondered what I'd just said and tapped her chin in thought. "Trouble? Like, what kind of trouble?" she asked.

"Brianna, if you let the dogs out of their cage, they can get into all SORTS of trouble! Okay?"

"So, do you mean trouble like tearing up the pillows, digging up Mom's plant, and pooping in Dad's favorite chair?" she asked casually, and then batted her eyes all innocentlike.

I turned and stared at my little sister in disbelief.

"Brianna! Don't tell me you let the dogs out of their cage?!" I groaned as I slammed my book shut.

There was just NO WAY I was going to finish my homework while babysitting ~~eight~~ NINE unruly animals.

"Okay! If you DON'T want me to tell you that I let the dogs out of their cage, then I WON'T! Can I have a cookie?" Brianna quipped.

OMG! I was SO mad at Brianna that I wanted to release all my frustration by screaming into a pillow.

But I couldn't, because the puppies were busily pulling every ounce of stuffing out of each one.

Cotton was scattered everywhere.

It looked like there had been a major snowstorm right in the family room.

That's when Brianna pointed and said . . .

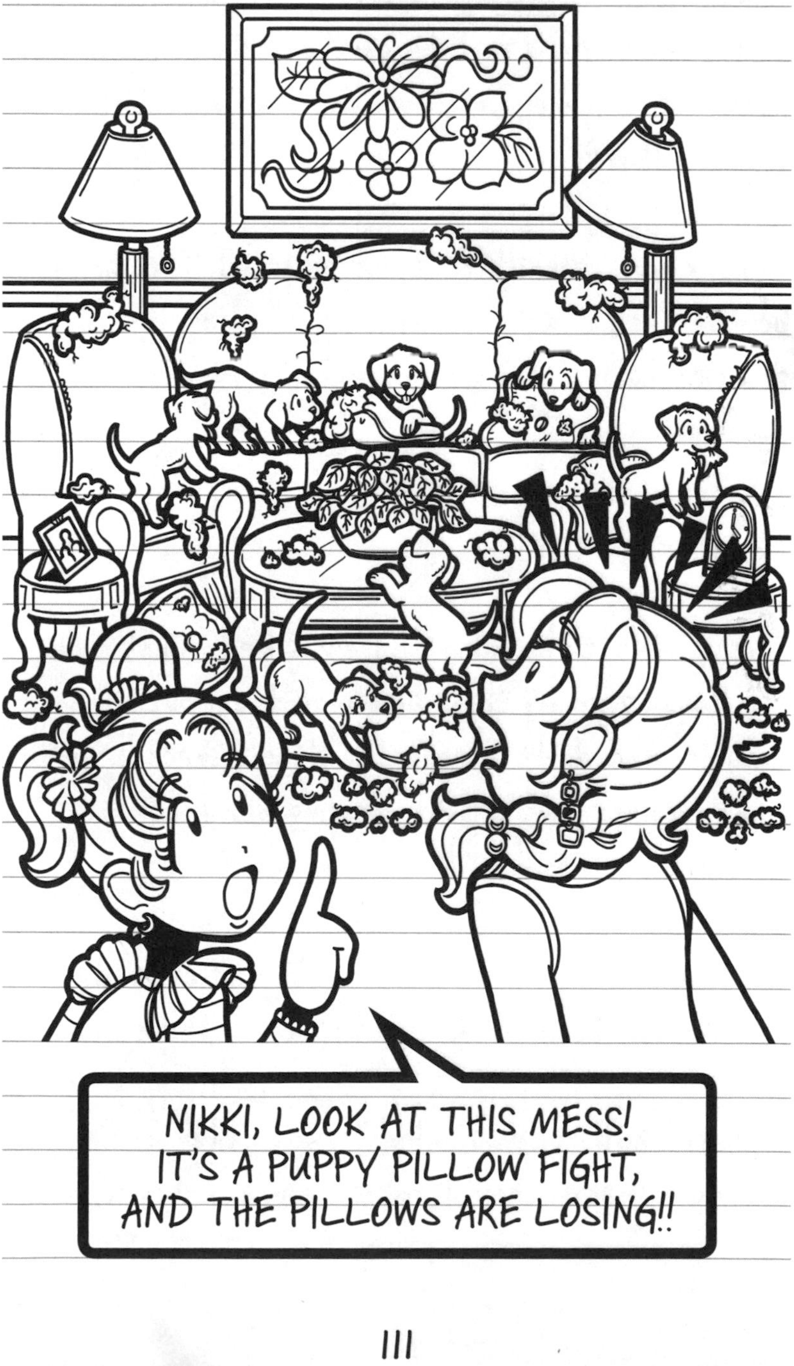
NIKKI, LOOK AT THIS MESS!
IT'S A PUPPY PILLOW FIGHT,
AND THE PILLOWS ARE LOSING!!

"JUST GREAT!!" I sighed. "Okay, Brianna! Here's your chance. You can take care of the dogs while I clean up this mess. If Mom and Dad see this, I'M DEAD MEAT!"

"Thank you, Nikki!" Brianna squealed. "I'm gonna be the best doggie sitter EVER! I got lots of practice taking care of Rover the fish a few weeks ago, remember?"

How could I forget?

"Please! Don't remind me!" I exclaimed. "Just take the dogs up to my room and keep them out of trouble. And don't forget the doggie snacks. You're going to need 'em!" I said, handing her a box of doggie doughnuts.

Brianna tossed one into her mouth and chewed. "YUM!! It's bacon-'n'-cheese! I LOVE these things!"

"They're not for you, silly! If you offer the pups a doggie snack, they'll follow you anywhere."

"Oh! I knew that!" Brianna grinned sheepishly. "Who wants a doggie snack?!" she asked, waving one in the air.

The dogs immediately stopped unstuffing the pillows and happily scampered up the stairs after Brianna and the doggie snack.

I have to admit, it was really nice to have a little "me time" away from Brianna and the dogs.

Frantically restuffing and sewing pillows while pricking my fingers bloody was actually a lot EASIER than trying to entertain eight rambunctious dogs and one bratty little sister.

But forty-five minutes later, as I was finishing up, I was suddenly overcome with paranoia.

At first I thought I was feeling faint due to the loss of blood.

But I couldn't exactly put my finger on it.

Probably because they were numb from being poked with the needle over and over.

Something was just . . .

WRONG!

Finally I figured it out.

"It's quiet. TOO quiet!" I muttered to myself. "Brianna is up to something!"

That's when I raced toward the stairs.

"Brianna! What are you doing with the dogs?!" I yelled on my way up. But there was no reply. "You'd better answer me, or else. . . ."

At the top of the stairs I found a sign, sloppily written in red crayon.

It was Brianna's handwriting!! . . .

Qwiet Pleez!
Welcome to
Miss Bri-Bri's
Paw Spa

There was yet another sign farther down the hall that said . . .

Of course, I decided to totally ignore her VERY
RUDE and unprofessional signs.

I had a good mind to report PAW SPA to the Better Business Bureau. But I digress. . . .

I followed the sound of classical spa music toward Brianna's bedroom.

That's when I noticed that Mom's battery-powered candles gently lit the hallway, while the floor had been sprinkled with flower petals for dramatic effect.

"Wow. Brianna really went all out for this make-believe spa," I thought. "The pink rose petals are actually a nice touch!"

But she didn't stop at just the roses. A few feet down the hall she had scattered lilacs and gardenias.

"Wait a minute. . . ." I frowned. "Where did she get these?!" For some reason, they looked awfully familiar.

Okay, I was starting to get nervous.

Near my bedroom door I saw scattered leaves, shrubbery, twigs, and . . . roots?!

Which made me VERY worried.

But I totally lost it when I saw the fresh dirt and confused worms scattered over Mom's new rug!

Brianna's bedroom door was locked, so I pounded on it with my fists.

"BRIANNAAAAAAAAA!!!!" I screamed. "I can't believe you completely MUTILATED Mrs. Wallabanger's prizewinning flower garden!!"

That's when a strange little woman wearing fake-diamond cat-eye glasses, a long scarf, a kiddie paint apron filled with Mom's spa essentials collection, six-sizes-too-big red heels, and way too much makeup and jewelry very cautiously opened Brianna's door and poked her head out.

She glared at me, scrunched up her nose, and hissed . . .

ME, BEING SHUSHED BY A
STRANGE LITTLE WOMAN!

I couldn't believe my eyes! It was . . .

Miss Bri-Bri ☹?!

Also known as Madame Bri-Bri, Fashionista Hairstylist to the Stars.

And now, apparently, the owner of the trendy new PAW SPA for non-"hoomans"!

She stared at me as I stared at her.

I knew right then and there that I was in for a . . .

VERY!

LONG!!

NIGHT!!!

☹!!

"SHHHHHH! Zis eez a relaxation spa, dah-ling!"
Miss Bri-Bri scolded me. "Did you not understand
zee sign?!"

"First of all, don't you dare SHUSH me! I'm the one
in charge here!" I shot back. "Second of all, your
signs were barely legible! I hate to break it to you,
madame, but you can't spell worth BEANS!"

"Sorry, I know nothing about zee beans that you
speak of. Miss Bri-Bri eez very busy, dah-ling!
Unless you are a puppy with le spa reservation,
I must ask you to leave. We enforce a strict 'no
hoomans allowed' policy! Read zee sign, please!"

Then she slammed the door right in my face. BAM!!

"Miss Bri-Bri! Er, I mean . . . BRIANNA, I'm about
three seconds from going APE CRAZY on you if
you don't open this door!" I growled. "ONE!! . . .
TWO!! . . . THREE!! . . ."

Suddenly the door was flung open.

"Dah-ling! Please! You MUST calm down. Or I'll
be forced to call SECURITY. BUT if you agree
to keep all of zee flowers you saw in zee hall
a big SECRET, then Miss Bri-Bri will give you a
DISCOUNT on le peanut butter facial! Deal?! Yes?!"

I could not believe Miss Bri-Bri was trying to
BRIBE me!

She could NEVER buy my SILENCE after
completely DESTROYING poor Mrs. Wallabanger's
prized flower garden next door!!

Although, that DISCOUNT on a facial DID sound
like a pretty good deal!

I LOVE going to the spa and getting those
fancy-schmancy treatments. But I digress. . . .

"For your information, spas have ALMOND SCRUB
facials! NOT peanut butter facials!" I corrected
Miss Bri-Bri. "And PLEASE don't tell me you

opened Dad's gallon container of natural no-salt, no-sugar peanut butter that he was saving for his birthday and put it on the dogs' faces?"

"Okay, then! Miss Bri-Bri will NOT tell you she opened zee big birthday bucket of natural peanut butter! But she NEVER, EVER put a drip of zee peanut butter on zee dogs' FACES!" she exclaimed. "What kind of a spa do you think this eez? So please! Do not worry about zat, dah-ling!"

"Thank goodness!" I muttered to myself, and breathed a sigh of relief.

"Today we have a special on zee FULL-BODY peanut butter massage. So I put zee peanut butter ALL OVER zee DOGS' BODIES," Miss Bri-Bri announced proudly. "Now zee dogs eez very relaxed! SEE?"

I looked behind her and gasped!

Holly and her seven puppies were puke brown and covered in peanut butter. . . .

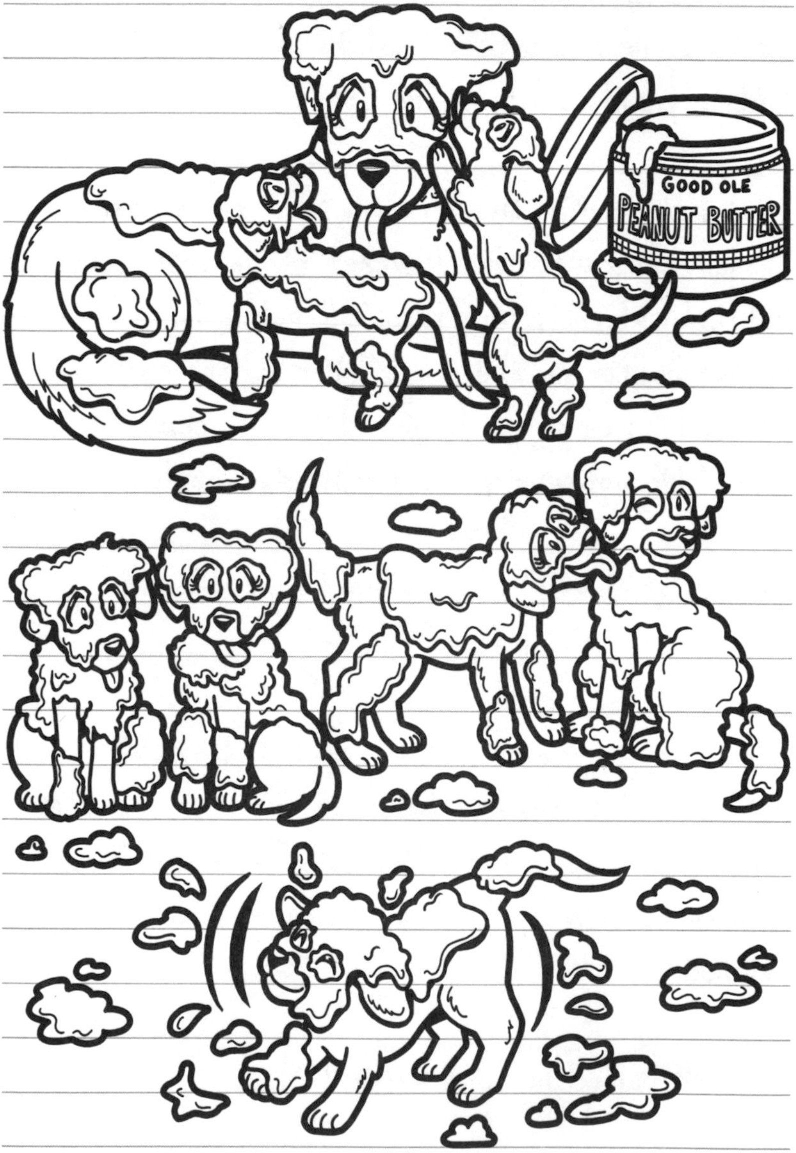
GOOD OLE
PEANUT BUTTER
DOGGIES AT THE PAW SPA!

"OMG! What have you done?! These dogs are COMPLETELY covered in Dad's BIRTHDAY peanut butter!!" I shrieked hysterically.

"Bah! Nonsense!" Miss Bri-Bri waved her hand at me dismissively. "I make zee dogs booty-ful. If zee dogs don't look good, I don't look good."

"Admit it, Miss Bri-Bri. You totally screwed up. These dogs look like some furballs that a giant cat coughed up after eating 139 peanut butter cookies," I complained. "Are you even a licensed spa professional?!"

"No need to be rude, dah-ling!" Miss Bri-Bri huffed. "Zee situation eez under control! My spa assistant-in-training, HANS, has prepared a special bath. All zee peanut-butter-covered dogs will be squeaky clean very soon. HANS! Please come clean zee dogs! NOW!"

I couldn't help but roll my eyes when she mentioned her assistant, HANS!

I will NEVER, EVER forget that guy!

Hans the TEDDY BEAR was the assistant on duty at SALON BRIANNA the day Miss Bri-Bri accidentally chopped off my ponytail back in February!

And he's an INCOMPETENT IDIOT!!

But WHATEVER!

Personally, I didn't care if the TOOTH FAIRY was going to help SANTA CLAUS give these dogs a bath.

As long as they were CLEAN, back in their CAGE, and HIDDEN in my room before Mom and Dad got home from the movie!

Miss Bri-Bri and I herded Holly and her puppies into the bathroom to put them into the tub for a quick bath.

That's when I realized we had three very BIG problems:

1. Her poorly trained teddy bear assistant, HANS, was floating upside down in the tub.

2. The tub wasn't filled with water. It was filled with . . .

MUD?!!!

AND

3. It wasn't just ordinary mud. The smell of that steaming cesspool was foul enough to peel the baby ducks right off the bathroom wallpaper!

"Brianna! WHY is there MUD in this bathtub?!" I screamed. "And why does it smell like something DIED in the mud and is STILL in there rotting?"

"*Wee! Wee!* Dis mud eez made of zee finest, filthiest dirt, hand—selected from Mrs. Wallabanger's MANURE compost pile by Miss Bri—Bri herself," she boasted. "You will not find another mud bath like it anywhere in zee world, dah—ling!"

ME, GAGGING AT THE HORRID
STENCH OF MISS BRI-BRI'S
MANURE AND MUD SPA BATH!!

OMG! The hot mud and manure bath smelled so bad, it actually singed my nose hairs.

It was like I could actually TASTE it.

"EWW!!" I gasped, and plugged my nose. "That's it, Brianna! I'm shutting you down!" I yelled. "This pretend spa is CLOSED. Sorry! But this has to be in violation of at least a dozen city health codes!!"

"But, Nikki, I'm NOT finished yet!" ~~Miss Bri-Bri~~ Brianna whined. "After the mud bath, Hans was going to give the dogs a jelly manicure. See?" She held up a jar of grape jelly and a plastic spoon.

"WHAT are you talking about? It's a GEL manicure, NOT a jelly manicure!" I corrected her. "Now get your teddy bear out of this tub so I can clean up this STINKY mess!"

"Hans? HANS!! Get out of that tub or you're FIRED!!" Miss Bri-Bri screamed as she grabbed his leg and tugged on him really hard.

THIS is what happened. . . .

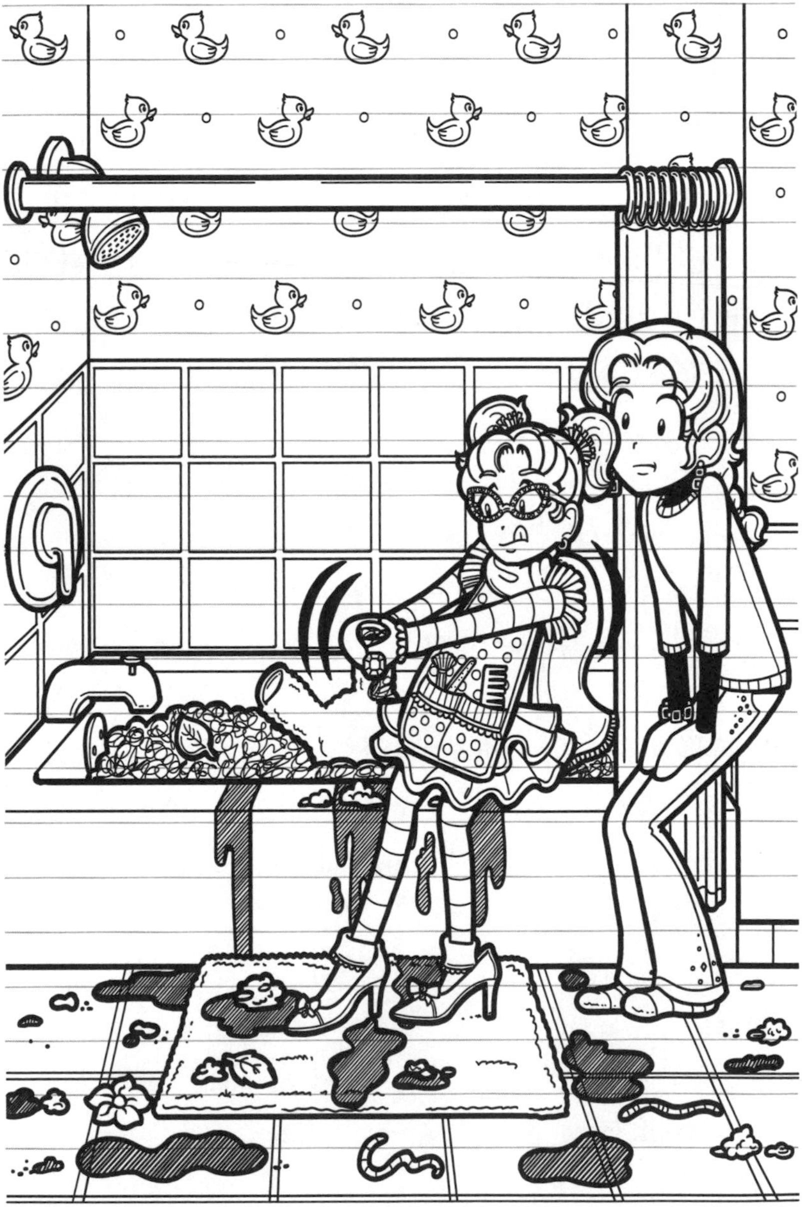

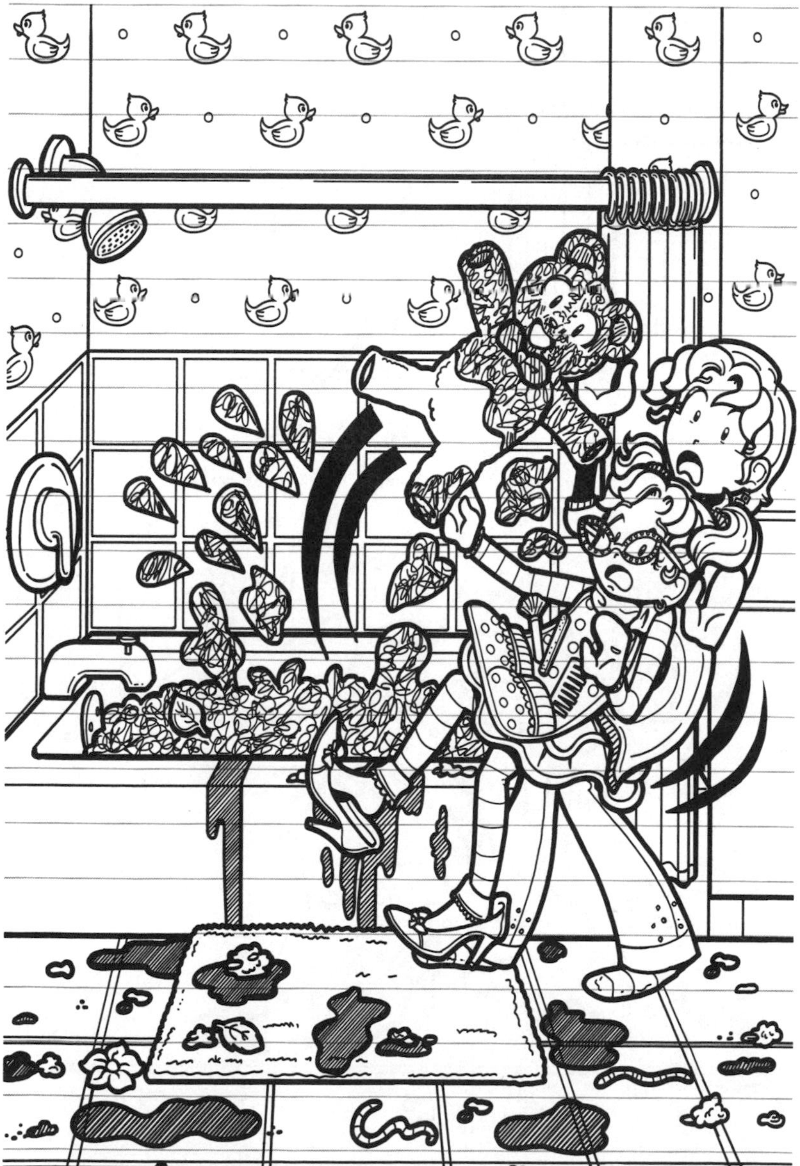

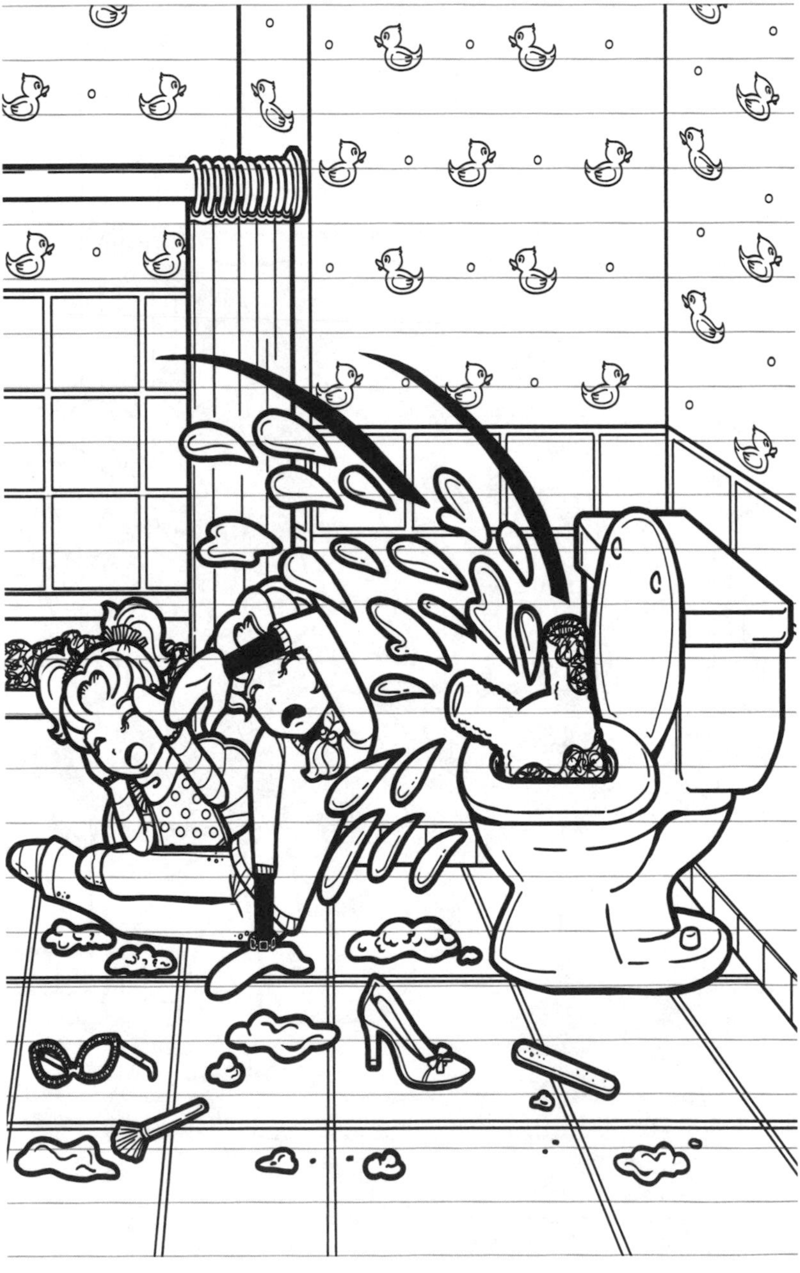

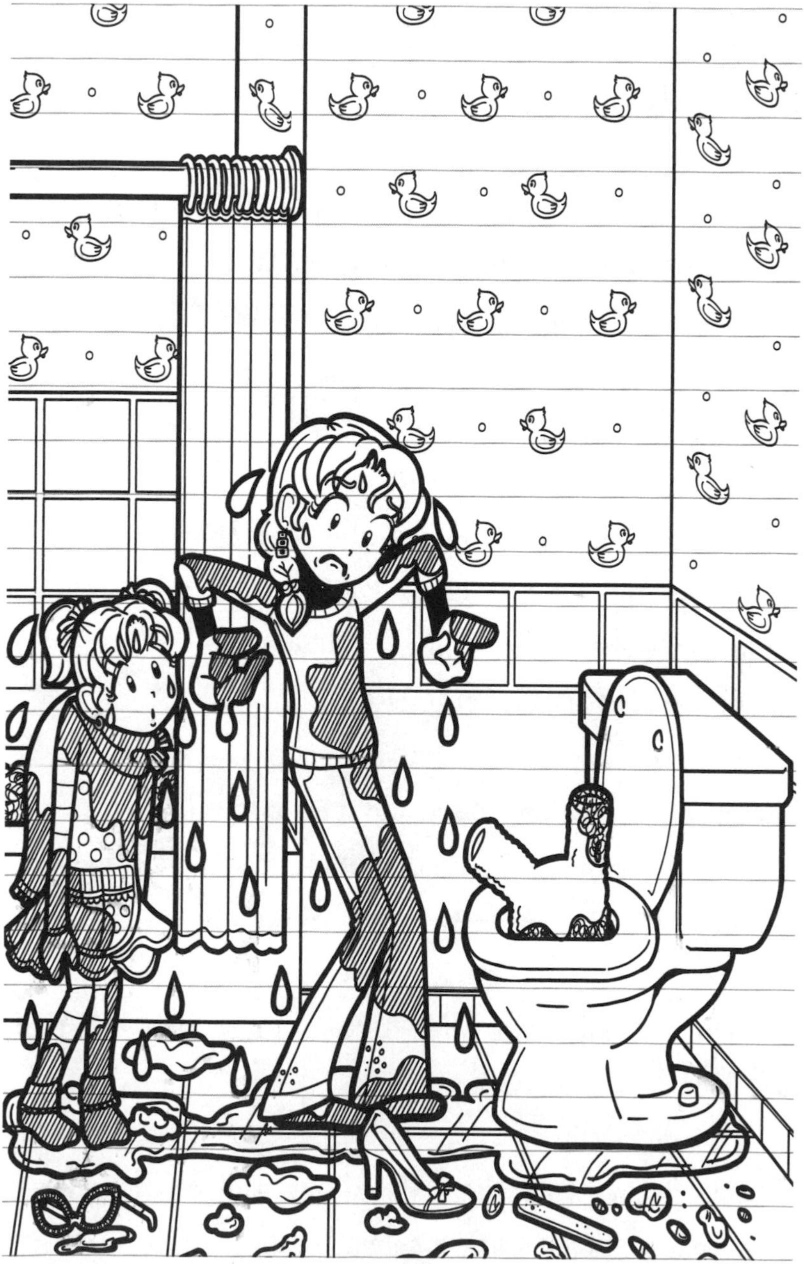

OMG! I couldn't believe it! Hans flew across the room like a torpedo and landed headfirst right in the toilet with a huge SPLASH!

Of course, Miss Bri-Bri and I totally FREAKED OUT because thanks to Hans, NOW we were dripping with manure and TOILET WATER!

EWWWWWW ☹!!! . . .

And by the time Brianna and I had chased down the dogs and herded them BACK into their cage, we were covered with manure, toilet water, and PEANUT BUTTER ☹!!

Surprisingly, taking care of the EIGHT dogs has NOT been my most difficult task. It's been taking care of ~~Miss Bri-Bri~~ Brianna!

Sorry, but all night she's been acting like a PACK OF WILD DOGS ☹!!

The last time I checked, Hans was still floating in the toilet. Which wasn't so bad, considering the fact that the toilet was ten times more sanitary than that manure mud bath!!

The dogs were FILTHY.

The bathroom was FILTHY.

And even Brianna and I were FILTHY.

There was just no WAY I could clean up all this FILTH before my parents got home.

Unless they were coming home in two weeks!!

My mom and dad were going to FREAK when they discovered not ONE dog, but EIGHT sticky, peanut-butter-covered dogs hiding inside their FILTHY house!!

I was a complete FAILURE!! And the WORST pet sitter EVER!!

Although, judging from the looks of Brianna, I was probably an even WORSE babysitter ☹!

So I decided to do what any normal responsible teen would do when faced with EIGHT dogs and ONE bratty little sister covered in manure, toilet water, and peanut butter.

I flopped down in the middle of the bathroom floor . . .

Closed my eyes . . .

And burst into TEARS!!

☹!!

I don't know exactly how long I'd been lying on the bathroom floor crying. I just remember hearing the doorbell ringing and wondering three things:

1. Why Mom and Dad were home so early from the movie theater.

2. Why they were ringing the doorbell instead of using their key to the front door.

AND

3. Whether they were going to ground me until my SENIOR year of high school or my FRESHMAN year of college.

Finally, ~~Miss Bri Bri~~ Brianna poked her head in the bathroom and told me what I already knew.

"Nikki, you better come downstairs quick! Someone is at the front door ringing the doorbell!" she exclaimed. "And if it's Mom and Dad, I'm going to go lock myself in my bedroom and play Princess Sugar Plum. But if they're REALLY mad, just tell them I ran away. Okay?"

I could NOT believe Brianna was just going to throw me under the bus like that! This whole thing was HER idea! Miss Bri-Bri's PAW SPA was a HOT MESS!!

DING-DONG! DING-DONG! DING-DONG!

JUST GREAT ☹! I could tell Mom and Dad were mad just by the way they were ringing the doorbell.

Still covered in toilet water, manure, and peanut butter, I sadly trudged downstairs to answer the door. All I could really say to my parents was that I was truly sorry, I had learned my lesson, and I would NEVER, EVER lie to them or hide anything from them AGAIN!!

I slowly opened the front door and was completely shocked to see . . .

. . . BRANDON?!

"BRANDON!! OMG! WHAT are you doing here?"
I gasped.

"Nikki, are you okay?" he asked, looking panicked. "I called your cell to see how things were going with the dogs. And, well . . . this really weird lady with a thick accent answered. She said you couldn't come to the phone because you were really mad about the peanut butter and mud and you were crying in the bathroom! She said something about hands being in the toilet and you closing her pa's spa! None of it made any sense! And then she just HUNG UP on me! It was so . . . BIZARRE!"

"WHAT?!" I sputtered.

I was SHOCKED! Brianna had actually answered MY cell phone and TALKED to Brandon?!!

I could NOT believe that girl was putting ALL my personal business in the STREETS like that!

Brandon continued. "I thought I had the wrong number, so I called back again. The same lady answered and told me not to call her again or she was contacting the cops. Anyway, since I was

right in the neighborhood working on a project,
I thought I'd just drop by to make sure everything
was okay! You and the dogs ARE okay, right?!
That lady really had me worried. And, um . . .
what's that SMELL?! PEW!!" he said, blinking his
eyes really fast like the odor was stinging them
or something.

Sorry, but I was NOT about to tell Brandon
the truth. That he had trusted me with the dogs
and I was a COMPLETE and UTTER FAILURE
as a pet sitter ☹!

So I decided to just LIE about how I'd read in
Teen Thing magazine that washing dogs in peanut
butter and manure compost killed all fleas (within
ten miles!) and gave them really shiny coats.

And yes! It had turned out to be a bit messier than
I had anticipated.

So I was in the process of cleaning (the dogs, my
little sister, Hans the teddy bear, and half of
the entire upstairs).

Then I decided to change the subject.

"So, Brandon, you said you were in the neighborhood?"

"Yeah. I was actually right next door in the white house. My good friend Max Crumbly and I are working on our project for the science fair. It's due tomorrow."

"That house?" I asked, surprised. "You were at Mrs. Wallabanger's?!"

"Yeah, Mrs. Wallabanger is Max's grandmother! Our project is called Using Distillation to Turn Dirty Water into Clean Drinking Water."

"Wow, Brandon! Our bio teacher mentioned the science fair. Your project sounds really complicated."

"Actually, it's not. It involves taking dirty water and turning it into clean drinking water. With enough research, one day this process could help provide clean water to Third World nations. Anyway, for our project to work, we need to use dirty water occurring naturally in the environment."

"That's totally amazing!" I gushed.

"We planned to use dirty runoff water from Mrs. Wallabanger's compost pile. But we just discovered that it's gone. So it looks like we might not be entering the science fair after all."

"Wow! What happened?" I asked, concerned.

"I know it sounds hard to believe, but it looks like someone vandalized her backyard and stole her compost. They also took a few of her prized flowers. Max's grandma insists her archfrenemy, Trixie Claire Jewel-Hollister, is behind it. They've been rivals since high school. Mrs. Wallabanger has been winning first place in all the local flower shows lately, and she says Trixie Hollister is a rich, spoiled, jealous SORE LOSER."

I was almost sure that Hollister lady was probably MacKenzie's grandmother or grandaunt.

I felt bad they were blaming her, but I didn't want to throw Brianna under the bus either.

"Well, I'm really sorry to hear you and Max might not be entering the science fair because— Wait a minute! I think I just might have some manure—I mean, COMPOST—lying around that I don't need!"

Brandon looked surprised. "You do?! Really?! Wow, that's great news! Can we borrow some for our project?"

"Actually, you can have ALL of it! I was planning to get rid of it anyway. But I'll need a little help, if you guys don't mind."

So I cleaned the FILTHY TOILET.

Brandon cleaned the FILTHY BATHTUB (he really liked Miss Bri-Bri's "SPA MUD").

And his friend Max cleaned the FILTHY DOGS in Mrs. Wallabanger's backyard. . . .

MAX, GIVING HOLLY AND
THE PUPPIES A BATH!

Brandon introduced me to his good friend Max Crumbly. He was nice, friendly, smart, and, ALMOST as CUTE as Brandon! SQUEEEE ☺!!

NIKKI, MEET MY GOOD FRIEND MAX CRUMBLY! HE'S MRS. WALLABANGER'S GRANDSON!

Brandon said Max is a really good artist (like ME!) and attends South Ridge public middle school just down the street.

They both thanked me for helping them out with their science project and invited me to attend.

Anyway, by the time my parents got home from the movie, everything and everyone was squeaky clean and fast asleep!

Yes, I admit that the evening was a COMPLETE DISASTER!!

WHY did I EVER think I could take care of EIGHT dogs when I could barely keep a PET ROCK alive?!

But, in the end, everything worked out just fine!

Maybe Miss Bri-Bri's full-body peanut butter massage DID relax the dogs. They've been quiet as mice all night.

I just hope tomorrow will be a lot less DRAMA!

Mom and Dad are chaperoning an all-day field trip to the Westchester Zoo for Brianna's class. So the three of them will already be gone by the time I get up.

I'll just let the dogs romp, play, and nap in my bedroom (with their pee-pee mat) until I get home from school.

THEN, by the time my family is back from the field trip, Brandon will have picked up the dogs and taken them to Chloe's house, and my pet sitting duties will be successfully completed!

Which means I will have kept EIGHT dogs right under my parents' noses for twenty-four hours without them EVER suspecting a thing!

Am I NOT an EVIL GENIUS?!

MWA-HA-HA-HA!

Well, I'd better get some sleep!

☺!!

AAAAAAAAAAAAAAAH!!!

(That was me screaming in TERROR!)

At first I didn't know if I was actually dreaming or awake. I was praying the very horrible THING I saw was just a really bad nightmare!

I had awakened, showered, and gotten dressed. Then I'd taken care of Holly and her pups.

They were in my room playing and romping around when I went downstairs to grab breakfast and head off to school.

WARNING! This is the scary NIGHTMARE part!

Just like the ~~victims~~ people in those horror movies, I was supposed to be home alone!

So, I totally FREAKED when I walked into the kitchen and saw . . .

ME, IN SHOCK MOM IS STILL HOME,
WHEN SHE WAS SUPPOSED TO BE GONE!

I was like, "Um, good morning, Mom! So . . .

WHAT ARE YOU DOING HERE?!!"

Mom looked at me kind of strange. "Well, right now I'm making a cup of coffee."

"What I meant was, aren't you and Dad supposed to be gone all day? You know, chaperoning Brianna's class at the zoo?"

"Actually, it was canceled due to a forecast of thundershowers. And since I've already taken the time off from work, I decided to just stay home and relax."

"WHAT?! You're staying HOME?!! ALL DAY?! Are you SURE?!" I gasped.

"Yes, I'm sure! Honey, are you feeling okay? You kind of look like you just saw a GHOST or something!"

"Actually, Mom, I felt just fine until I walked into this kitchen. Now I wanna throw up! Er, what

I mean is . . . YES! I'm not sick at all. And I'm feeling very fine, actually," I babbled.

Okay, I had a HUMONGOUS problem!

There was no way I could leave the dogs in my bedroom with Mom in the house all day.

And even if I stashed them in the garage, she'd probably stumble upon them out there, too.

I needed to get them out of the house, and FAST!!

If one of the puppies even SNEEZED, there was a good chance Mom would hear it, all alone in the house with eight dogs ☹!

Unlike my SCHOOL, which was busy, crowded, and practically a ZOO!

That place was usually so NOISY, I could BARELY hear my own THOUGHTS!

As crazy as it sounded, I didn't have a choice but to take the dogs to SCHOOL with me!!

Or face the WRATH OF MOM ☹!!

I texted Chloe and Zoey and made them aware of the impending CATASTROPHE!

They told me to remain calm and meet them at the side door near the school library ASAP.

But I STILL had to resolve TWO very minor, yet important, questions.

Since no one orders pizzas for breakfast at 7:00 a.m., Queasy Cheesy was still closed and their drivers were not available. So HOW was I supposed to convince my mom or dad to drive me and EIGHT dogs to school? Without them EVER discovering the, um, DOGS?

That's when I suddenly remembered that my BFFs and I were meeting near the LIBRARY. And it had lots and lots of BOOKS.

So I grabbed a marker, paper, blanket, and wagon and created the perfect doggie disguise. . . .

BOOKS
FOR
LIBRARY

I had barely finished covering the dog cage with Brianna's old baby blanket when I suddenly heard the garage door open.

Brianna's eyes got as big as saucers, and she looked like she was about to wet her pants.

When I turned around, Dad was standing there with a mug of coffee, STARING right at the DOG CAGE.

OMG! I was SO startled, I almost lost my biscuits-'n'-gravy breakfast.

Dad looked at the dog cage and then at me and then back at the dog cage again. I thought for sure I was BUSTED!!

Until he said, "So, Nikki, it looks like you're going to need help getting those library books to school. I'll go unlock the van and load you up."

I was speechless. And very happy ☺!!

My dad had volunteered to take me and the ~~dogs~~ "library books" to school!

"Thanks, Dad," I said. "I really appreciate it."

"That's a BIG load of books! Where did you find them, Nikki?" he asked, taking a swig of coffee.

"Actually, someone left them all on a doorstep, and I've been taking care of them until I could find them a home. Well, A HOME in our school LIBRARY, of course!" I explained nervously.

Dad unlocked the van door and went back into the house to let Mom know he was driving me to school.

I quickly wheeled the "books" out to the van, and Brianna helped me load everything inside before he returned.

As Dad pulled out of the driveway, I turned on the radio and blasted his favorite golden oldies music station so loud I thought my ears were going to bleed.

Luckily, the loud music made it almost impossible for Dad to hear the dogs bark.

BUT if he had glanced at the "library books" behind him, he would have been in for a really big surprise. . . .

My heart was pounding in my chest like the bass to my favorite rap song as I adjusted the blanket to cover the curious puppies.

WHAT WAS I THINKING ☹?!!

I must have been suffering from TEMPORARY INSANITY when I came up with the RIDICULOUS idea to bring eight dogs to school.

I was already DREADING my day at school!

And it hadn't even started yet.

☹!!

As planned, Chloe and Zoey were waiting for me by the side door near the library.

"Hi, guys!" I jumped out of the van, grabbed their arms, and led them to the back of the van so Dad couldn't hear.

"So, will you help me unload the, um . . . . BOOKS?!"

"Books?" Zoey asked. "What books?"

I gave her and Chloe a wink.

"Oh! THOSE books! Sure!" Zoey said.

"Nikki, what happened to the DOGS?" Chloe blurted out. "Are they still in your bedroom?! I thought you were bringing them with you to school today and—

Zoey gave Chloe a swift kick to shut her up.

"OW! That hurt!" Chloe whined.

"Need any help, girls?" Dad asked, standing right behind us.

OMG! He nearly scared the Kibbles 'n Bits out of us! I really wished he'd STOP sneaking up on people like that.

He opened the back door of the van and reached for the load of "library books."

"NO!" I said, grabbing his hand. "I mean, no thanks, Dad! We got this. Mrs. Peach would fire us from working at the library. You understand, right?"

"Not really. But fine." He shrugged. "You kids are more nervous than a wet cat! It's like you're trying to smuggle mice into a cheese factory or something!"

Not quite! We were trying to smuggle eight dogs into a middle school.

Chloe, Zoey, and I looked at each other and giggled nervously.

Not because his joke was funny, but because Holly's tail was hanging out from under the blanket. . . .

SO, GIRLS! UM . . . WHAT'S SO FUNNY?

GIGGLE! GIGGLE! GIGGLE! GIGGLE!

After Chloe, Zoey, and I unloaded the dog cage and wagon, we waved good-bye to my dad, and wheeled the "books" into the library.

"Keeping the cage in here might be risky!" I said, looking around. "What if Mrs. Peach sees the sign and thinks it's actually library books?"

"Maybe if we change the sign to 'GARBAGE,' she won't look?" Chloe reasoned. "But then she might throw it out. I know! How about 'SNAKES'? Then she wouldn't go near it!"

"No! We should hide the dogs in a safe, top secret place that only WE know about. Like, hmmm . . . ," Zoey said, tapping her chin.

Suddenly we all had the exact same idea. . . .

"THE JANITOR'S CLOSET!" we yelled excitedly.

We quickly wheeled the cage down the hall to the janitor's closet. . . .

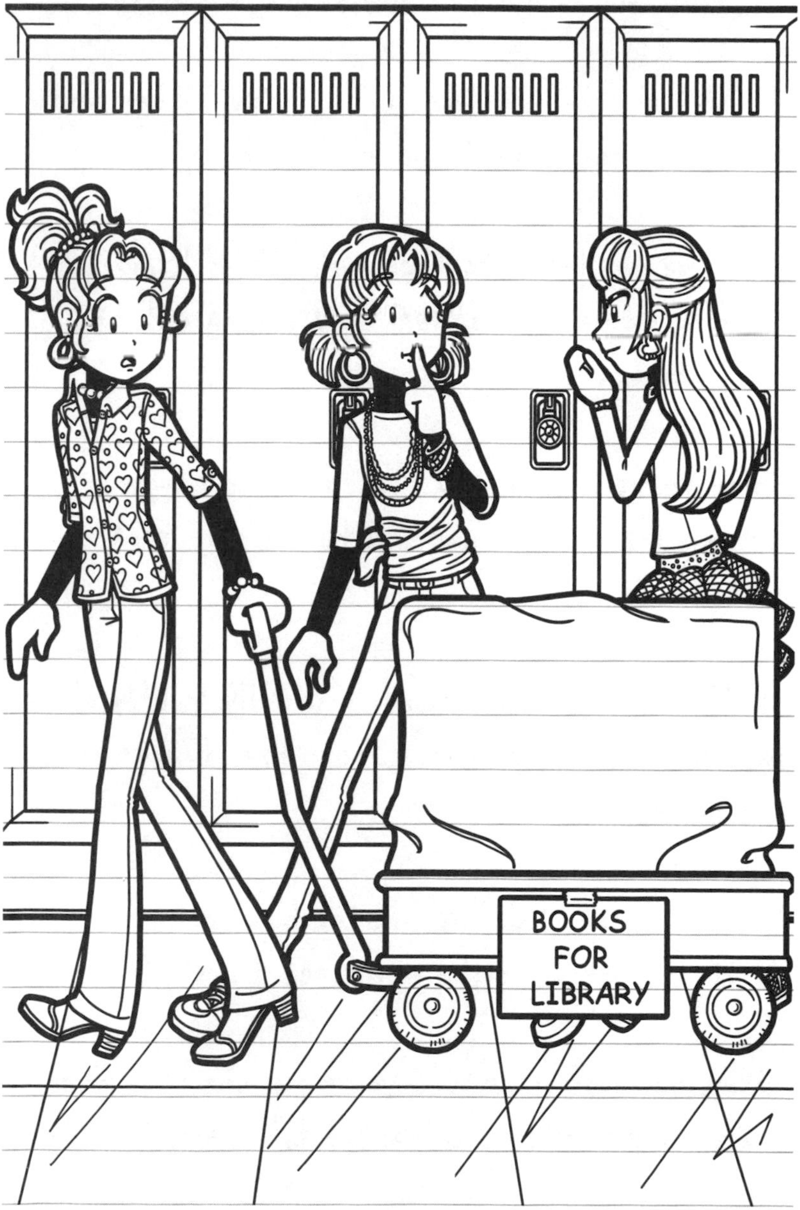
BOOKS
FOR
LIBRARY

We rolled the cage inside and closed the door.

"I just hope the dogs aren't too noisy," Zoey said, pulling off the blanket and folding it up.

"Well, we can listen to them with this," I said, reaching inside my backpack and pulling out the baby monitor.

Chloe turned it on and placed the receiver part on top of the cage and handed the speaker part to me.

All the puppies were resting, and Holly quietly stared out at us, probably curious about her strange new surroundings.

"Look!" Chloe said. "Her water bowl is empty. I'll fill it back up so she won't get thirsty!"

"Okay, but just make sure you close the cage when you're done so they can't get out," I said, turning the volume on the receiver to high.

I wanted to make sure I could hear every little sound. Then I placed it inside my backpack.

We said good-bye to the dogs, carefully closed the janitor's closet door, and headed for our lockers.

Today, students were reporting to their homerooms for first hour instead of our regular classes.

This worked out for us since we were all in the same homeroom.

"Whatever you do, act natural and stay cool," I whispered to Chloe and Zoey as we took our seats.

"And just think POSITIVE thoughts!" Zoey whispered.

"Yeah, because if someone finds those dogs in the janitor's closet, I'm POSITIVE we'll be KICKED

out of this school like a SOCCER BALL!" Chloe
added in a whisper.

I was like, thanks a lot, Chloe!

After hearing her positive thought, I was more
WORRIED than EVER!!

☹!!

The classroom was so quiet, you could hear a pin drop. Then . . .

BOOM! SPLASH! BARK! YIP-YIP! CRASH!

The loud noises from my backpack startled me so badly I practically jumped out of my seat. OMG! It sounded like pure puppy pandemonium!

I immediately regretted that I'd turned up the volume of the baby monitor so high.

I ALSO immediately regretted that I hadn't checked to make sure Chloe had CLOSED that CAGE DOOR after refilling Holly's water bowl ☹!!

Every single person in the room heard it, including Chloe and Zoey. I totally panicked.

My startled teacher stopped writing on the board, walked over to my desk, and gawked at me. . . .

ME, DISRUPTING THE CLASS WITH MY
VERY NOISY "STOMACH SOUNDS"

"Nikki, are you okay?!" she asked, looking very concerned.

"Uh . . . have you ever been so queasy that your stomach sounds like seven dogs fighting in a utility closet?! That's totally me right now!" I grabbed my stomach and faked a very loud and painful moan.

My teacher shuddered at the thought.

"Actually, no, I haven't. Thankfully!" she muttered.

YIP-YIP! BANG! SQUEAL! BARK! CRASH!

"Sorry! But this could get really ugly!" I said, and then moaned really long and loud like a moose with a bad toothache.

Mostly I was trying my hardest to cover up the noise coming from my backpack.

But I don't think it was working.

"I'm really worried about you, Nikki! Did you maybe eat something that didn't agree with you?!" my teacher asked.

"Probably! Remember that blue cheese macaroni casserole from lunch yesterday? Only it was actually more of a moldy green color and smelled like fermented skunk spit? I ate THREE large bowls of it! UGH!!"

I watched as kids frantically scooted their desks out of my puking range.

Come on! Even if I really had eaten that stuff, they wouldn't need to move away like that.

Hey! They'd need to SWIM out of the room!

I'm just sayin'.

SQUEAL! BARK! CRASH! YIP-YIP!
BANG! GRRRR! BARK! YIP! CRASH!
BANG! CRASH!

A few kids were staring at me in horror, like I was possessed! By the DRUM SECTION of a small middle school MARCHING BAND!

What were those dogs doing in there?

Chasing BOWLING BALLS?! And playing fetch with the MOP BUCKETS?!

"OW! OW! OOOOOOW!" Zoey suddenly yelled like a coyote howling at the moon. "Teacher, I had too much of that MOLD-A-RONI—er, I mean, macaroni—too! I am SOOOO sick!"

Then Chloe joined in. "MOO! QUACK-QUACK! OINK-OINK! COCK-A-DOODLE-DOO!!"

Girlfriend was definitely overdoing the theatrics. She sounded like a barnyard at sunrise!

Then, for dramatic effect, I reenacted that infamous scene from that time MacKenzie threw up in French class!! . . .

CHLOE, ZOEY, AND ME,
PRETENDING TO BE VERY SICK!

OMG! That's when the entire classroom went completely nuts!

Everyone knows that puking can be contagious. It's probably never BEEN scientifically proven, but STILL!

At least four other kids were holding their mouths and starting to look really sick too.

Only, unlike Chloe, Zoey, and ME, THOSE kids were probably REALLY going to THROW UP ☹!!

Just one kid getting sick in class was SUPERgross!

EWW!!

But FOUR at the same time?!

Quadruple EWW!!

I definitely didn't want to be around when THAT happened.

"OH NO!" my teacher cried, suddenly realizing the gravity of the situation. "All three of you are IMMEDIATELY excused! Now HURRY, before your lunch comes back to say hello all over my clean floor! GO! Please! Just GO!"

It was quite clear the teacher had heard about the MACKENZIE PUKE FIASCO. Because THIS lady was NOT having it in HER classroom!!

Chloe, Zoey, and I exchanged glances.

In spite of our very bad acting skills, our plan was obviously working!

"Tank you, Teacher!" I grimaced.

Then I grabbed my backpack, and the three of us staggered out of the room all queasylike.

But as soon as I closed the door, we sprinted down the hall toward the janitor's closet like we were competing in a 100-meter dash. . . .

CHLOE, ZOEY, AND ME, RACING DOWN
THE HALL TO CHECK ON THE DOGS!

As we sprinted down the hall, it felt like the janitor's closet was two miles away.

By the time we reached it, we were pretty frantic and completely out of breath.

I cautiously opened the door, and the three of us peeked in.

OMG!

I couldn't believe the HUGE mess those dogs had made!

It gave a whole new meaning to that popular old-school song "WHO LET THE DOGS OUT"!

But mostly, we couldn't believe all the FUN the puppies seemed to be having.

Everything in there had been . . .

Chewed.

Gnawed.

Chipped.

Scratched.

Torn.

Tattered.

Shattered.

Shredded.

Or broken.

But thank goodness!!

The DOGS were all in one piece and doing just fine. . . .

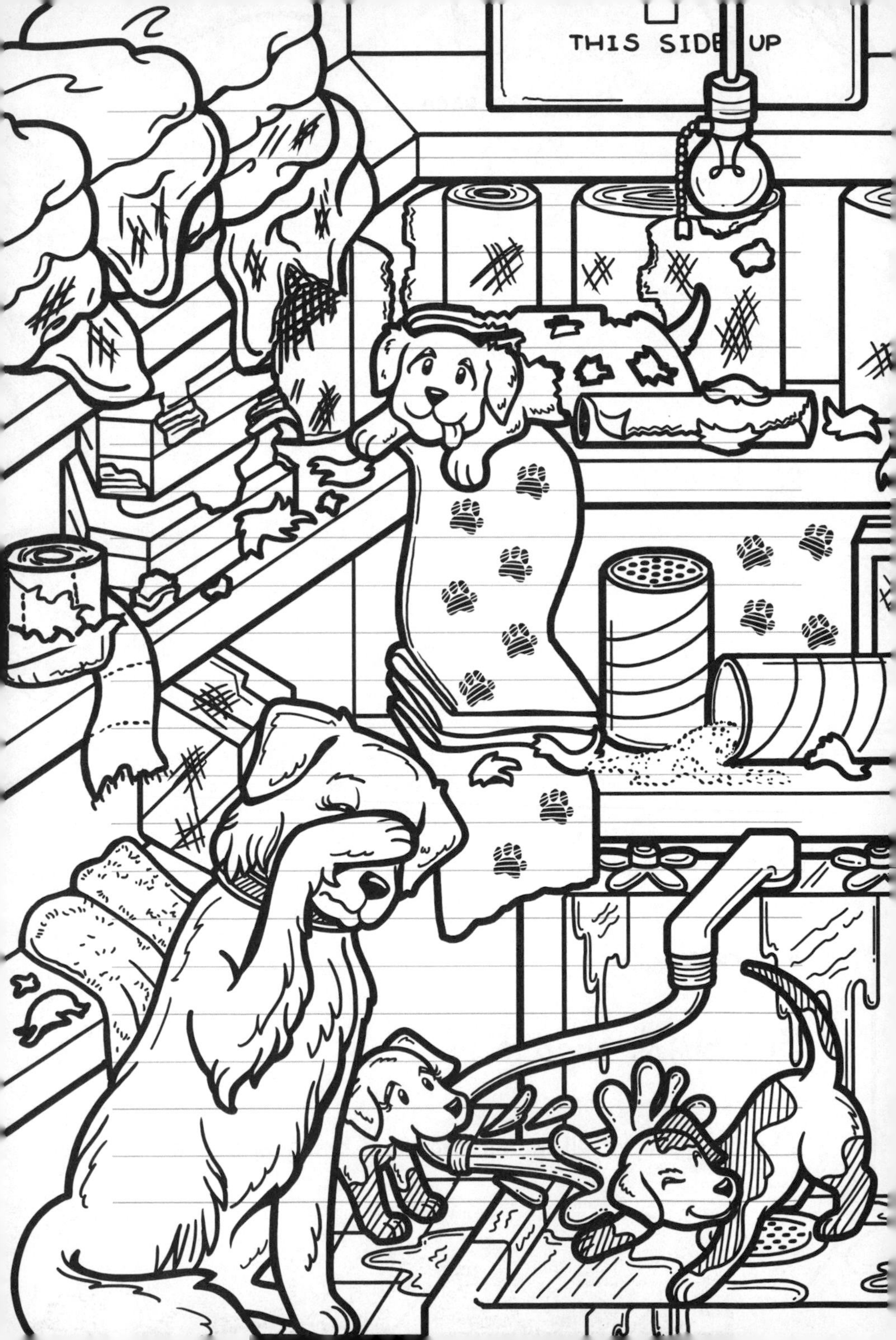
THIS SIDE UP

TOILET PAPER
TOILET PAPER
TOILET PAPER
TOILET PAPER

There were mounds of powdered detergent, puddles of dirty mop water, soap suds, and shredded toilet paper everywhere! Two puppies were playing with the water hose in the mop sink.

I'm no dog whisperer, but I think Holly was totally embarrassed by her puppies' antics.

It was hard to believe that such LITTLE puppies could make such a HUMONGOUS mess. It actually looked like they'd thrown a wild house party in there and TRASHED the place!

"It's going to take at least an hour to clean this mess up," Zoey groaned. "We'll just have to come back and tackle it during lunch when we have more time."

"Yeah, I know. But we need to get the dogs out of here first," I muttered.

"Where else can we put them?" Chloe asked. "Mrs. Peach will be in the library all afternoon, so THAT'S not an option!"

"Guys! I have a REALLY CRAZY idea." I grinned.
"And I'm pretty sure it will probably work!
Or WRECK our lives and get us EXPELLED
from school."

"Wow, sounds just perfect!" Zoey replied
sarcastically, and rolled her eyes.

"Just hear me out," I said. "Principal Winston is
out of the building all day today for a meeting
at the high school. Right?! Well, since he's not
in his office—"

"I know!" Chloe interrupted excitedly. "We can just
SKIP SCHOOL for the rest of the day and take
the dogs to MY house! Since he's not here, he won't
know and we won't get EXPELLED! Right?!"

"Not exactly, Chloe. Just LISTEN, okay?" I said,
mildly annoyed. "We could hide the dogs in his office,
and no one would EVER find them. That's because
absolutely no one would even DARE go in there
without his permission. Unless they were REALLY,
REALLY STUPID or something!!"

Zoey slapped her palm on her forehead. "DUH!! Am I the ONLY one who sees the IRONY here? Sheesh!"

"There's an IRON in here?!" Chloe asked, looking around. "Where is it? Like, who would iron clothes in a janitor's closet? Oooh! I know! The JANITOR, right?"

"Chloe! I said 'IRONY'!" Zoey sighed.

"I know. I heard you the first time. But I still don't see any iron," Chloe muttered.

"Chloe! There's NO iron! Trust me," I said.

"I didn't THINK so! Tell that to Zoey," Chloe grumped.

"Come on, Zoey!" I argued. "If you have a better idea, let's hear it."

"Actually, I think Chloe's really stupid idea of SKIPPING school is BETTER. And LESS risky," she grumbled.

I just rolled my eyes at Zoey and didn't say a word.

Finally Zoey sighed. "Nikki, if you think your plan will actually work, let's try it! We definitely CAN'T keep the dogs in here!"

"Great!" I smiled. "Now, listen carefully, guys. My plan is VERY, VERY simple! ALL we have to do is SNEAK the dogs into Principal Winston's office, keep them from totally TRASHING the place like they did the janitor's closet, make sure no one accidentally discovers them, and then SNEAK back into his office at the end of the day and take them home! Like, how hard can THAT BE?!"

Chloe and Zoey just folded their arms and stared at me.

"So that's the plan. Do you guys have any questions?" I asked happily.

"Yes, I think Chloe and I have the same question," Zoey muttered. . . .

Okay, I wasn't quite expecting THAT question. But hey, that's Chloe and Zoey. You gotta LOVE 'EM!

Coming up with the idea to hide the dogs in
Principal Winston's office was pretty easy.

However, figuring out HOW to get the dogs into
Principal Winston's office was the hard part. So this
was the MASTER PLAN!

Chloe was going to lock herself in a bathroom stall
and ~~do her very bad imitations of various barnyard
animals~~ pretend to be sick.

We'd ask the office secretary to check on Chloe
because we were worried about her.

While the secretary was out of the office, Zoey
and I would simply roll the dog cage into Principal
Winston's office and close his door.

Since his office was in a separate corridor from the
noisy main office, it would be pretty hard to hear
the dogs unless they made a huge racket.

Then, at the end of the day, we'd simply ask
to retrieve our box of "library books" that had
inadvertently ended up in Principal Winston's office
instead of in the library.

I knew my plan was far-fetched, ill-conceived, and
very risky. But I didn't have any other options.

Except to confess everything to my parents ☹!

We were scoping out the office when the door
opened and the secretary walked down the hall and
disappeared into the teachers' lounge.

We couldn't believe our good luck ☺!

With the office temporarily unattended, we'd have the
PERFECT opportunity to sneak the dogs into the
principal's office.

We grabbed the wagon and rushed into the office,
only to discover some GOOD news and some BAD
news. The BAD news was that there was a student
office assistant on duty ☹!

But the GOOD news was that it was our friend
MARCY ☺!! . . .

GOOD MORNING, NIKKI, CHLOE, AND ZOEY! SO, HOW CAN I HELP YOU ALL?

STUDENT OFFICE ASSISTANT

OUR GOOD FRIEND MARCY IS THE STUDENT
OFFICE ASSISTANT ON DUTY!

"What's up, Marcy?" I said. "We have a really big favor we'd like to ask you! It's kind of a secret!"

She stared at the wagon behind us with a puzzled look on her face. Then she read the sign and blinked in disbelief.

"OMG! I can't believe you guys would actually do something like this! And you expect me to keep it a secret?! The entire school needs to know what you're doing!" Marcy screeched excitedly.

It seemed really clear from her over-the-top reaction that she must have spotted a puppy peeking out from under the blanket, or a wayward tail wagging or something.

JUST GREAT! We were so BUSTED ☹!!

Chloe, Zoey, and I went into panic mode.

"Listen, Marcy, I can explain all of this! Just give me a chance! Please!" I pleaded with her.

"When the secretary returns from her break, I'm sure she's going to be as shocked and surprised by what you're doing as I am! Of course she'll inform Principal Winston the minute he gets back," Marcy continued.

"Actually, Marcy, it looks like you're pretty busy here. So we really should be getting back to class!" Zoey exclaimed. "Have a nice day!"

But Chloe totally lost it.

"OH NO!! Now we're going to get EXPELLED from school and our parents are going to KILL us!!" she shrieked hysterically as she grabbed her stomach. "UGH! I think I'm going to be SICK! For real! Cock-a-doodle-doo! Moo! Oink!"

"Okay, Marcy, I won't bother to explain what we're trying to do! So just forget we were even here!" I said in frustration.

"No! You don't have to explain anything. It's quite obvious. You're collecting book donations for the library! AGAIN! Right?! You guys are unbelievable! Our school is really lucky to have dedicated students like you so willing to give of yourselves. Principal Winston should give each of you the Student of the Year award! I'M just SO proud and honored to be your friend!" Marcy gushed.

"NOW, WHAT CAN I DO TO HELP?!"

Chloe, Zoey, and I glanced at each other and giggled nervously.

WHEW!! That was close!

I was glad Marcy had offered to help us.

But after her glowing compliments, asking her to ABUSE her position as student office assistant by helping us smuggle eight dogs into Principal Winston's office had suddenly gotten a lot harder!

I had chosen to get involved in all of this to try to help Brandon save Holly and her puppies.

But to involve innocent people like my BFFs, and now Marcy!

I felt like a SNAKE! A dishonest, manipulative, and very DESPERATE snake!

I didn't have a choice but to call my parents and tell them everything. BEFORE I got my friends and myself into serious trouble.

"Thanks, Marcy! So does this mean we're NOT getting EXPELLED for sneaking Holly and her puppies into school?!" Chloe blurted out.

Zoey gave Chloe a swift kick to shut her up.

"OW! That hurt!" Chloe grumped, and shot Zoey a dirty look.

"Puppies?! Did you just say PUPPIES?!" Marcy gasped excitedly. "OMG! I LOVE puppies! I've been begging my parents to get one, like, FOREVER! Where are they?! Can I see them?! PLEEEEEEASE!!"

Okay, that's when I decided NOT to call my parents and tell them about Holly and her puppies.

S-s-so what if I'm a s-s-s-sneaky s-s-s-snake ☺!

I told Marcy all about Holly and her pups and how we were helping Brandon save them.

Then I let her have a peek at them. . . .

ME, SHOWING MARCY THE DOGS!!

Marcy didn't seem the least bit disappointed that our library books were actually dogs.

And after hearing about our doggie dilemma, Marcy agreed that Principal Winston's office would make the PERFECT hideout until the end of the school day ☺!!

Especially since Principal Winston wasn't expected to return during school hours.

"Marcy, we really appreciate you offering to help, but are you SURE you want to do this?! If we get caught, you could get detention—or worse!" I warned her.

"Well, to be honest, I'm not that worried about detention. I just don't want to be demoted from office assistant to team uniform assistant. The sweaty guys on our wrestling team are the worst! After practice their uniforms smell like Dumpster juice and swamp gas!" she complained. "ICK!!"

"Marcy, we totally understand if you're having second thoughts about helping us," I said sympathetically.

"Yeah, we wouldn't ask you to do something this crazy and risky unless it was for a really good cause," Zoey explained.

But Chloe was no help whatsoever. She made a sad pouty face like she was about to cry.

"Marcy, just look at these cute wittle faces!" Chloe squeaked in baby talk. "Don't you just wuv these wittle doggies! Yes, you willy do!"

Almost as if on cue, all eight dogs gave us the biggest, saddest, most angelic puppy-dog eyes EVER!

"Awwwwww!" the four of us gushed.

"Poor wittle puppies are willy, willy sad!" Chloe said glumly.

"Okay, guys! I'm in!" Marcy sniffed. "I'd have to be completely HEARTLESS to say no to those cute wittle faces. I already wuv 'em! I willy do!"

Chloe, Zoey, and I were so happy, we gave Marcy a group hug!

"Thanks, guys!" Marcy smiled. "The secretary will be coming back from her break any minute now. We need to get these dogs moved into Principal Winston's office right away!"

I guess the fact that we were ACTUALLY about to hide eight dogs in the principal's office must have FINALLY sunk in or something.

Because suddenly my heart started to pound. And my palms got SUPERsweaty. And my stomach started to feel very queasy for real!

I took a deep breath, nodded, and calmly said, "Okay, Marcy, let's do this!"

But inside my head I was totally FREAKING OUT!

I wanted to run out of the office hysterically screaming. . . .

I just hope my KA-RAY-ZEE plan actually works!

☹!!

Marcy cautiously turned the knob to Principal Winston's office and . . .

CLICK!!

OMG! We nearly jumped out of our skins!

"AAAH!!" Chloe shrieked, and grabbed my arm.

Okay, so THAT was the LOUDEST doorknob click EVER!

But STILL!

There was no need for Chloe to act like she'd just seen an ax murderer or something.

"CHLOE! Let go of my arm!" I whisper-shouted.

"Sorry!" she muttered. "I'm just a little jumpy, okay?"

The four of us nervously tiptoed into the dark office, wheeling the dog cage behind us.

For some reason, it felt really creepy in there.

Like at any second some nightmarish creature was going to crawl out of the shadows, grab us with its long, bony claws, and do something really HORRIBLE to us!

You know, like . . .

ENROLL US IN SUMMER SCHOOL!!

EEEEEEEEEK ☹!!!

Marcy stopped in the middle of the room. "SHHHHH!! Do you guys hear that sound?!"

I definitely heard it!

KNOCK–KNOCK!

KNOCK–KNOCK!

"OH NO!" Zoey gasped. "I think someone is knocking on the door! We're DOOMED!"

"That's not the door! It's Chloe's KNEES!!" I said, rolling my eyes.

"Hey, I already told you I was a little jumpy!" Chloe snarked. "This place feels like a haunted house or something! Does anyone have a flashlight?"

"That's it! I can't handle this!" Marcy cried. "I'm going to do what I should've done in the beginning!"

She turned and headed straight for the door.

I could NOT believe she would just panic and abandon us like that.

"Wait, Marcy! Come back!" I whisper-shouted.

"Well, it looks like she'd rather smell funky wrestler uniforms than hang out with us puppy smugglers!" Chloe grumbled. "TRAITOR!"

CHLOE, ZOEY, AND I FREAK OUT AS
MARCY HEADS FOR THE DOOR!

When Marcy reached the door, she stopped.

Then she hit a switch on the wall, and bright lights flooded the room.

Chloe, Zoey, and I blinked in surprise.

"There! Isn't this a lot better?" Marcy said as she opened the curtains on a window. "I don't know about you guys, but the darkness was giving me SERIOUS goose bumps!"

Chloe's fright subsided as we looked around.

The office was a lot less Temple of Doom–looking with the lights on.

Actually, it was kind of on the boring side.

Cheesy-looking certificates hung on the walls, a bookcase was filled with dusty books, and a clock sat next to a framed family photo. A big candy jar sat on his desk along with stacks of papers.

I couldn't help but shudder. Hopefully, today was the FIRST and the LAST time I'd be hanging out in the principal's office.

I folded the doggie blanket and placed it in the wagon.

All the dogs had cuddled together and were about to take their midmorning nap.

"I think they're still exhausted from that big party they had in the janitor's closet. So they'll probably just sleep the rest of the day. You won't even know they're here," I assured Marcy.

"Great! I'll come back to check on them every hour between classes. And if there's a problem, I'll text you, Nikki," Marcy explained. "Otherwise, just meet me here after school to pick them up."

"Thanks, Marcy! You're a lifesaver!" I said.

Suddenly Marcy froze.

"SHHHHHHH!! I hear another strange sound!" she whispered.

SMACK-SMACK! SMACK! SMACK! SMACK-SMACK!

I definitely heard it too!

Alarmed, Marcy, Zoey, and I stared at the door.

Were those footsteps?

OMG! What if the secretary was coming in to place Principal Winston's mail on his desk and discovered us in here?

I quickly searched the room for a hiding spot.

"Maybe we should hide in that closet!" I shouted quietly.

"Hey, guys! Don't FREAK OUT! It's just ME," Chloe giggled.

We turned around to see her smacking loudly on the last few pieces of chocolate in Principal Winston's candy jar. . . .

CHLOE, SNARFING DOWN CANDY
FROM PRINCIPAL WINSTON'S CANDY JAR!

"Sorry if I sound like a pig! But those mini candy bar thingies are DELISH!"

Evidently, in the sixty seconds we had our backs turned, Chloe had somehow crammed most of the candy bars from that big candy jar into her dainty little mouth!

Seriously! How did she do that?

Does her jaw UNHINGE when she eats, like those huge snakes on the Animal Planet TV shows?!

Anyway, in spite of Chloe's noisy feeding frenzy, the dogs had finally fallen asleep.

Marcy turned out the lights, and we rushed back to the main office.

And just in time, too.

As we headed into the hall on our way to class, the secretary held the door open for us.

"Have a nice day, girls!" She smiled.

"You too!" we said, and smiled back at her.

Anyway, thank goodness the dogs are safely hidden away in Principal Winston's office, where no one will find them.

Now all I have to do is just survive the rest of the school day, which is about FIVE hours.

How HARD can THAT be?!

Chloe, Zoey, and I gobbled down our lunches as fast as we could.

Then we snuck out of the cafeteria and rushed straight to the janitor's closet as planned.

OMG! The room looked like it had been hit by a Category 3 hurricane.

It seemed like it was going to take us FOREVER to clean up the HUGE mess those dogs had made. Although my BFFs and I HATED cleaning our bedrooms and LOATHED putting dishes in the dishwasher, we somehow managed to finish up by the time lunch was over.

How?!

We donned our rubber gloves and combined our strength to become the powerful SUPERHEROES known as . . .

Unfortunately for us, we also ended up SMELLING like the janitor's closet ☹!

Which is a combination of soap, toilet bowl cleaner, and musty, moldy MOP!

EWW ☹!!

Anyway, Marcy has been checking on the dogs every hour between classes, and she said she'd text me if anything came up. I haven't heard from her, so NO news is GOOD news ☺!

Maybe this whole dog sitting thing is going to work out after all.

Just a few more hours left until the end of the school day.

SQUEEEEE!!!
☺!!

FRIDAY—1:00 P.M.
IN BIOLOGY CLASS

The big science fair is today after school, and students are already setting up in the gym. My bio teacher had a flyer posted on her wall. . . .

Since half of the students in our biology class were in the gym setting up for the fair (including Brandon ☺!), our teacher told us we could spend the hour quietly reviewing for our chapter test next week.

It was nice having the extra time to study bio, but to be honest, I was bored out of my skull.

Why study for the bio chapter test TODAY when I can just PROCRASTINATE and study for it NEXT WEEK?

Anyway, I just checked my text messages and didn't have any from Marcy, so the dogs must be doing okay ☺!

And school will be over soon!

BUT just in case there IS a problem, I wanted to be totally prepared.

So I decided to use my class time wisely and write an excuse generator, mostly just for fun ☺!! . . .

EXCUSE GENERATOR
FOR WHY THERE ARE EIGHT DOGS
IN PRINCIPAL WINSTON'S OFFICE

To: Principal Winston

From: Nikki J. Maxwell

Dear Principal Winston,

You are probably wondering why there are eight dogs in your office. So, please, allow me to explain.

But first, I sincerely want you to know that I'm just as:

☐ shocked
☐ confused
☐ hungry
☐ bald

as you are about this very troubling situation.

I was on my way to class this morning when
I thought I heard:
- ☐ scratching
- ☐ barfing
- ☐ singing
- ☐ "cock-a-doodle-doo"

at one of the exit doors.

I assumed it was just:
- ☐ a pizza delivery guy
- ☐ a circus clown
- ☐ a rabid squirrel
- ☐ a bloodthirsty vampire

trying to get in.

So I opened the door just a tiny bit to get
a quick peek. But before I could stop them,
eight dogs quickly ran inside.

I tried to catch them, but they were
faster than:
- ☐ lightning
- ☐ uncontrolled diarrhea
- ☐ a slug in an ice storm
- ☐ a race car driver with four flat tires

and they somehow disappeared down a hallway.

So I thoroughly searched every single:
- ☐ classroom
- ☐ toilet
- ☐ locker
- ☐ garbage Dumpster

but I STILL couldn't find them.

This made me so frustrated that I wanted to:
- ☐ eat a peanut butter, jelly, and pickle
  sandwich

☐ pick my nose
☐ do the hokey pokey
☐ take a bubble bath

and then sob hysterically.

The only place I HADN'T searched was your
office! And that was because I didn't want to
break any school rules and possibly risk getting:
☐ expelled from WCD
☐ an after-school detention
☐ a severe case of diaper rash
☐ a zit on my nose the size of a raisin

which, unfortunately, would become part
of my permanent school record and possibly
prevent me from getting admitted to a
major university.

Sadly, I had no choice but to search for
the dogs in your office.

Of course, as soon as I found them there,
I immediately:
- ☐ wet my pants
- ☐ fainted
- ☐ took a selfie
- ☐ stepped in doggie poo

which was such a traumatic experience that
it will take me years to recover.

Fortunately, the dogs were merely:
- ☐ eating student report cards
- ☐ drinking out of the toilet
- ☐ chewing a hole in your leather office
  chair
- ☐ taking a nap

so your office was not heavily damaged.

I had just left your office to call Fuzzy
Friends Animal Rescue Center to pick up

the dogs and find them homes, when I
discovered you had returned and found the
dogs in your office.

I'll never again open our school doors for:
☐ eight renegade retrievers
☐ seven prissy poodles
☐ six yappy Yorkies
☐ five dorky Dalmatians and a partridge
   in a pear tree

because I have learned my lesson.

Sincerely,

NIKKI J. MAXWELL

☺!

FRIDAY—3:05 P.M.
IN THE SCHOOL LIBRARY

It's hard to believe a day that started so HORRIBLY WRONG is ending so PERFECTLY RIGHT ☺!

Chloe, Zoey, and I were working in the library as LSAs (library shelving assistants) when Brandon stopped by.

We both had been really busy with stuff and hadn't seen each other all day.

"Hey, Nikki! I just wanted to thank you again for that compost for my science project. I gave the leftovers to Mrs. Wallabanger, and she was thrilled. She plans to use it to fix her flower garden."

"No problem! I'm always happy to help." I smiled.

Then Brandon got SUPERserious. "But most of all thank you for helping me with Holly and her pups. You've been just . . . AWESOME!" he

gushed as he brushed his shaggy bangs out of
his eyes.

Then he, like . . . stared right into the . . . murky
depths of my . . . fragile but tortured . . . soul.

OMG! I thought I was going to MELT into a big
puddle of sticky goo right there at the front desk.

SQUEEEEEEE ☺!!

I decided to be perfectly honest with Brandon
because TRUE friendship is based on honesty, trust,
and mutual respect. Right?!

"Thanks, Brandon! I have to admit I've had some
challenging moments with the dogs. But overall things
have gone really well, and they've been a lot of fun!"

Okay, so maybe I wasn't COMPLETELY honest.

Yes, I know! I very conveniently left out the fact
that my mom had told me I COULDN'T dog sit but

I had done it anyway and kept the dogs hidden in my bedroom.

And I didn't mention how my mom had decided to stay home this morning, which meant I couldn't leave the dogs at the house as originally planned.

I also skipped the part about me bringing the dogs to school today.

And the fact that Chloe, Zoey, and I had hidden them in the janitor's closet.

And how Marcy had helped us smuggle them into Principal Winston's office while he was out for the day.

So I guess you could say I basically LIED to Brandon by NOT telling him things. Sort of.

But get THIS! He said he planned to thank me for all of my help by getting us cupcakes at the CupCakery sometime soon!

SQUEEEEEEEEE ☺!!

I was really happy to hear that news (and so were those nosy snoops Chloe and Zoey!) . . .

Anyway, in less than ONE hour, we'll be meeting Marcy to pick up the dogs from the principal's office.

And then Chloe will take over.

Chloe and Zoey are both really LUCKY because THEIR parents know about the dogs. So they won't have to sneak around or hide them in their bedrooms like I did.

I'm just happy I survived the past twenty-four hours! And so did ALL the dogs!

SQUEEEEEEEEEE ☺!!

I don't mean to brag or anything.

But I've been the . . .

PERFECT.

PET SITTER!!

☺!!

Okay!! MUST. NOT. PANIC ☹!!

I just got some text messages from MARCY!!

MARCY: Waiting for you guys in Winston's
office. Dogs are fine. See you soon.
ME: Great! At my locker waiting for
Chloe and Zoey. Should be there in about
2 minutes.
MARCY: BTW, dog water bowl is empty.
Is it okay to give them more water?
ME: Please do not open dog cage. So,
no water.
MARCY: Are you sure? They look thirsty.
ME: DO NOT OPEN DOG CAGE!!!!!!!!!!!!!!!!!!
MARCY: OOPS!! ☹!!
ME: What happened?!!
ME: Marcy?!!!!!!!!!!!!!!!!!!!!!!!!!
MARCY: HEEEEEEEEELP!!!

This is what happened. . . .

MARCY OPENS THE DOG CAGE ☹!!

I was about to rush off to rescue Marcy when I heard someone calling my name.

"NIKKI! Wait up! I need to talk to you!"

Brandon jogged up and leaned on my locker, completely out of breath.

"Whew! I just ran all the way from the gym to the library, and then here. But I'm glad I caught you before you left! I forgot to mention this earlier, but is anyone at your house right now?"

That's when I got another text from Marcy.

MARCY: Trying to put dogs back in cage. Impossible! Where are you guys?!

"Actually, Brandon, my mom is home right now. She didn't go to work today. Why do you ask?"

"Great! Since I have to be at the science fair until 7:00 this evening, I just sent the Queasy Cheesy driver to your house to pick up the dogs

226

and take them to Chloe's house. Is that okay?"

I just stared at Brandon with my mouth dangling open. "Wait a minute! You already sent the driver to MY HOUSE?!"

"Yes," Brandon answered.

"TO PICK UP THE DOGS?!"

"Yes."

"FROM MY MOM?!!!" I practically screeched.

"Is there a problem? I thought you said she was home," Brandon asked, a little confused.

"She is home! Er, I mean, she WAS! Actually."

That's when I got another text from Marcy.

MARCY: WHERE ARE YOU?!!!! The dogs are running around and getting into everything!! HELP!!!

"Um . . . my mom just texted me. She took the dogs . . . er, SHOPPING! They won't be back for at least an hour."

"Shopping? Really!" Brandon said. "Well, I'll just tell the driver to wait in the driveway until she gets back."

"NO! He can't! I mean, okay. But after shopping she plans to go to, um . . . the SPA!"

"Nikki, your mom is taking eight dogs shopping and to the spa?!"

"It's a DOGGIE spa! And it's run by Miss Bri-Bri. She's the lady you spoke to on the phone yesterday. They'll probably be there for, like, seventeen hours, so the driver definitely shouldn't wait!"

Then, Chloe and Zoey walked up.

"Hi, Nikki. Is everything okay?" Zoey asked.

"Yeah, you look a little flustered!" Chloe added.

"Well, things ARE a little crazy right now!" Brandon explained. "Nikki just gave me an update on the dogs. And some of it is almost unbelievable!"

"YOU TOLD BRANDON ABOUT THE DOGS?!!" Chloe and Zoey exclaimed.

"YES! I mean, NO! Sorry, I'm just really, really confused right now!" I muttered.

"Nikki told me the dogs aren't at her house right now," Brandon said.

"So you know all about us bringing the dogs to school today?!" Chloe laughed.

"And them completely trashing the janitor's closet?!" Zoey giggled.

"Nikki, why are you making those strange, ugly faces at us and pointing at Brandon?" Chloe asked.

"OOPS!" Chloe and Zoey mumbled.

That's when Brandon started to freak out. "Okay, wait a minute! Did you guys just say you brought the dogs to SCHOOL today?! And put them in the JANITOR'S CLOSET?!"

"No, we DIDN'T just say that," Chloe fibbed.

"Well, Nikki just told me her MOM was taking them SHOPPING and to a doggie SPA?!" Brandon said.

"YOUR MOM IS TAKING THE DOGS SHOPPING AND TO A DOGGIE SPA?!" Chloe and Zoey exclaimed.

"Well, yes! Of course she didn't!" I shrugged.

"Okay, Nikki! I'm really confused!" Brandon said, shaking his head. "If the dogs are NOT at your house OR in the janitor's closet OR shopping with your mom OR at the doggie spa, then WHERE in the heck ARE they?!"

Brandon, Chloe, and Zoey stared at me, like, FOREVER, waiting for my answer.

Suddenly Marcy came running down the hall, screaming at the top of her lungs! . . .

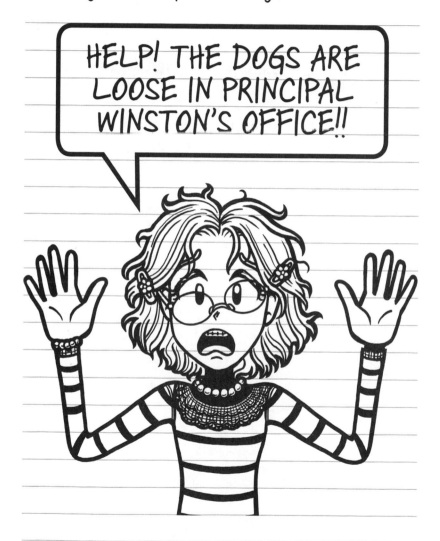

Which meant I DIDN'T have to answer Brandon's question, because MARCY did ☺!

"WHAT! The dogs are in Principal Winston's office?!! Are you guys SERIOUS?!" Brandon groaned.

"As serious as a HEART ATTACK!" we answered.

That's when the five of us frantically took off running to get to the principal's office!

☹!!

FRIDAY—4:09 P.M.
IN THE PRINCIPAL'S OFFICE

AAAAAAAAAAAAAHHHHH!!!
(That was me screaming.)

OMG! I was so ANGRY at myself!

WHY did I think I could secretly keep eight dogs in my bedroom? And then take them to school? And hide them in the janitor's closet? And then smuggle them into the principal's office?

WHAT was I thinking?!!!!

And just when I thought things couldn't get any worse, they did.

When the five of us finally arrived at the principal's office, we cautiously peeked inside. Unfortunately, we saw eight dogs running loose, trashing the office.

AND one very confused, ticked-off principal . . .

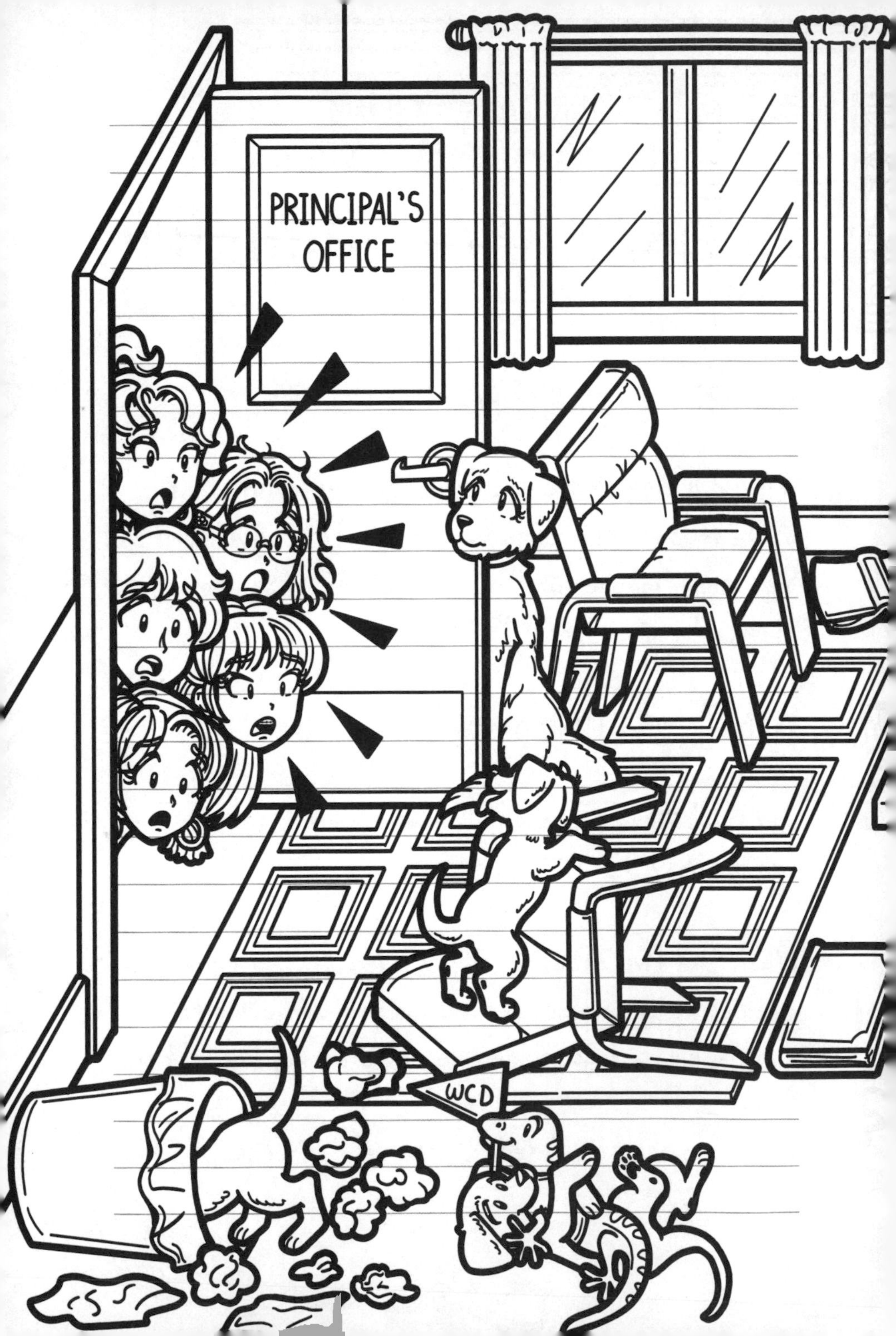
PRINCIPAL'S OFFICE
WCD

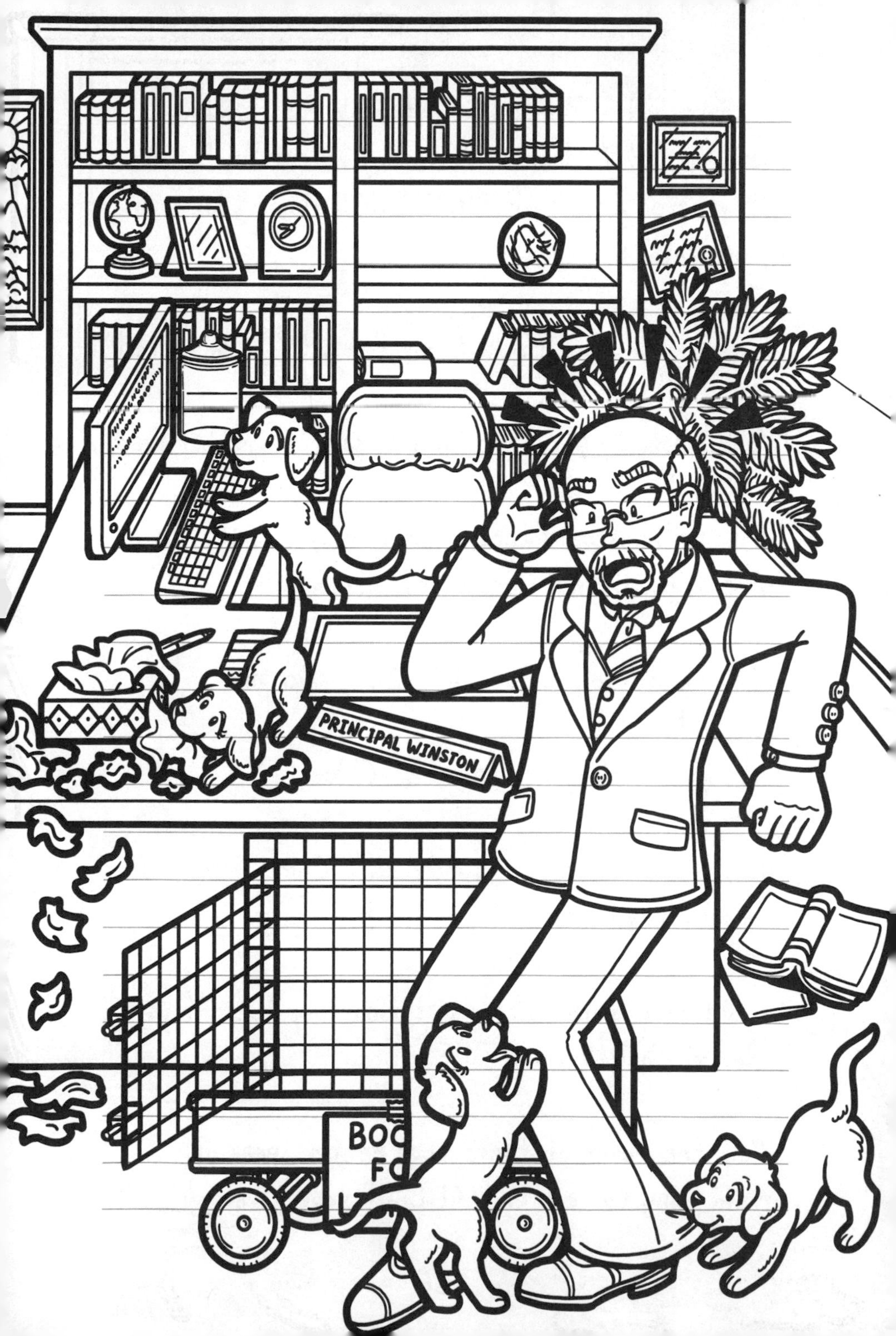
PRINCIPAL WINSTON

Of course, when Principal Winston saw us standing there, he totally lost it! "Can anyone explain to me WHY there's a pack of WILD DOGS running loose in my office?!" he yelled.

"I'm sorry, sir! But it's ALL my f—fault!" I stammered.

"No, it's actually MY fault!" Marcy said, hanging her head.

"Principal Winston, I accept total responsibility for these dogs," Brandon admitted solemnly.

"Well, I was involved too, sir!" Zoey said glumly.

That's when everyone stared at Chloe.

"Hey, I just raided your candy jar!" Chloe shrugged. "I'm no puppy smuggler!"

I could NOT believe Chloe was throwing ALL of us under the bus like that!!

"Well, the owner of these dogs better speak up, or I'm going to be calling ALL of your parents!!"

It got SO quiet you could hear a pin drop. Then we heard a friendly voice in the doorway. . . .

EXCUSE ME, PRINCIPAL WINSTON, BUT THESE DOGS ARE PART OF MY SCIENCE FAIR PROJECT, AND SOMEHOW THEY ESCAPED! I'M REALLY SORRY ABOUT THAT!

IT WAS MAX CRUMBLY?!!

Of course, everyone was shocked to see him standing there. And poor Principal Winston was so confused, he didn't know WHO to believe. Until Max called Holly over and all eight dogs tackled him and smothered him with kisses. . . .

BOOKS
FOR
LIBRARY

Max introduced himself to the principal and told him he attended South Ridge Middle School.

He went on to explain that his science fair project with Brandon was Using Distillation to Turn Dirty Water into Clean Drinking Water.

And it involved taking dirty runoff water from compost, and bathwater (from the dogs), and turning it into clean drinking water.

Principal Winston was VERY impressed with both Max AND his science project. And apparently, so were Chloe, Zoey, and Marcy. For some unknown reason, all THREE of them suddenly got a severe case of the giggles.

I could NOT believe that they were actually FLIRTING with Max like that.

Anyway, while Principal Winston chatted with Max, Brandon started to gather up the dogs and put them back in their cage, and Chloe, Zoey, and Marcy tidied up the office.

MAX, DISTRACTING PRINCIPAL WINSTON
WHILE WE DID DAMAGE CONTROL!

As Max was about to leave, he and Brandon
exchanged glances.

Then Brandon cleared his throat.

"Actually, Principal Winston, if it's okay with you,
maybe we can help Max with the dogs."

"Yeah, we definitely wouldn't want them to get
loose during the science fair!" I added.

"That's a good idea!" Principal Winston agreed.
"So why don't all of you help Max keep an eye
on them!"

"Now that I think about it, I'll probably just take
the dogs home before they cause any more trouble,"
Max reasoned.

"Actually, Max, I like THAT idea even better!"
Principal Winston chuckled.

Brandon grabbed the wagon, and the six of us got
the heck out of there!

Once we had made it out into the hall with the dogs, everyone was SO relieved! We actually high–fived each other.

"Nice work, Crumbly!" Brandon exclaimed.

"OMG! I thought Principal Winston was going to call our parents for sure!" I sputtered. "I almost peed my pants!"

Of course everyone laughed at my silly joke.

"Which reminds me," Brandon said, "I still need to call the driver and tell him NOT to pick up the dogs from your house, Nikki!" He took out his cell phone. "I'll just have him come to the school instead!"

Anyway, I managed to survive yet another CATASTROPHE! Thanks to MAX CRUMBLY!

That guy is actually pretty COOL!

☺!!!
...

FRIDAY—4:45 P.M.
AT CHLOE'S HOUSE

Right now I'm so completely EXHAUSTED from all of the drama with the dogs that I could fall over!

After we left the principal's office, Chloe rushed home to get ready for the dogs.

And since Brandon had to be at the science fair, I agreed to help deliver them to Chloe's house.

I have to admit, I was SUPERrelieved that I DIDN'T have to HIDE them from my parents anymore.

It was a miracle I was actually able to keep the dogs hidden in my bedroom without them finding out.

After a very noisy trip with the dogs in a van, I anxiously rang Chloe's doorbell.

DING-DONG! DING-DONG! DING-DONG!

243

The first thing I planned to do when I got back home was relax in a warm bubble bath ☺!

No, wait! The upstairs bathroom still reeked of manure and peanut butter ☹. EWW!!

Okay. Instead, I'd just chillax by finishing up a watercolor painting I'd started last weekend.

But that was going to be difficult to do since the dogs had chewed a leg off my artist easel ☹.

Well, I could always lounge around in my comfy pj's and bunny slippers and just write in my diary ☺.

NOT! The dogs had accidentally peed on my pj's and chewed the ears off my bunny slippers ☹. So now they looked like big fuzzy rats (my bunny slippers, not the dogs)!

My thoughts were interrupted when someone finally answered the door. The person was wearing a surgical mask, surgical scrubs, and latex gloves, and was holding a can of spray cleaner. . . .

ME, WONDERING WHY CHLOE WAS
DRESSED SO STRANGELY?!

"Hi, Nikki. Yeah, it's me. Did you get my phone message? I'm really sorry," she said glumly.

I burst into giggles.

"Hey there, Doc McStuffins! Did I catch you in the middle of surgery?" I teased.

Chloe pulled down her face mask and glared at me.

"No, Miss Smarty-Pants! I sneezed and it freaked out my uncle. So now he's forcing me to wear this getup AND spray the room with disinfectant," she complained. "He's a total germophobe! He just got here a few hours ago and is refusing to go back to his condo because his next-door neighbor just adopted a . . . um, D-O-G!"

"WHAT?! Chloe, why did you spell 'dog'?"

"Shhhhh!" she hissed, and looked over her shoulder nervously. "That word will practically send my uncle into convulsions. So we have to be VERY careful what we say."

"Chloe! Who's at the door?!" I heard a man yell from the kitchen. "Please tell them they can't come inside without a face mask and latex gloves. We have enough germs in this house!"

"Just stop worrying, Uncle Carlos! Please!" Chloe answered, a little irritated.

He continued. . . .

"And if it's the mailman, please call the Centers for Disease Control! Heaven knows what deadly germs are living on those spit-covered envelopes people have licked that he carries from house to house. He's probably spreading the bubonic plague! I'm getting heart palpitations just thinking about it!"

"Uncle Carlos, it's just my friend Nikki," she replied. "PLEASE! Just chill out!"

"How can I NOT worry when you're standing there with the door open? Do you realize you're letting in dozens of airborne viruses every minute? No wonder I'm feeling really sick!" he complained as he sprayed the room. . . .

CHLOE'S UNCLE CARLOS IS
A LITTLE, UM . . . WEIRD!

"Sorry, Nikki. Just ignore him!" she whispered. "So, what's up?"

"Chloe, I HEARD that!" he yelled. "In spite of my nasal congestion and severe ear infection from my allergies, I can STILL hear!"

Chloe rolled her eyes in frustration.

"Um, actually, Chloe," I began, "I just came by to drop off these, um . . . eight packages . . . just like we discussed," I said awkwardly, and pointed to the dogs.

"So I guess you DIDN'T get the message I left on your cell phone," Chloe sighed.

"What message?" I asked. "I guess I didn't hear my phone ring. The dogs were SUPERnoisy on the trip over here."

Chloe cringed when I said the word "dogs."

"OOPS!" I muttered. "Sorry!"

"DOGS?!" her uncle gasped. "Did someone just say 'DOGS'?! Take them away before I break out in a rash! Oh no! I'm already starting to itch!"

"No, Uncle Carlos! Nikki said 'DAWGS'! It's just a slang word for 'friends,'" Chloe fibbed. "Hey, Nikki, can you help me out here?" she whispered, nudging my arm.

"Yo! Listen up, Chloe!" I suddenly exclaimed very loudly. "Me and my dawgs will be chillin' at Crazy Burger tonight. You down with that?"

Startled, the smallest puppy looked up at me and barked. Chloe and I both shushed her.

"Chloe! Did I just hear a DOG?!" her uncle yelled.

He coughed overdramatically. "Now I'm getting light-headed and short of breath! It's probably an asthma attack! Chloe, quick, call 911!"

"Uncle Carlos, you DON'T have asthma!" Chloe grumbled. "Besides, you've already made me call 911 three times in the past hour. They've probably blocked our phone number by now!"

"Then use your cell phone!" her uncle argued. "And just because I don't have asthma right now doesn't mean I won't get it later today!"

Chloe looked like she was about to lose it!

"How about I babysit the dogs and YOU babysit my uncle?" she mumbled under her breath.

"I HEARD that!" her uncle shouted again. "Are you SURE there are no DOGS in this house?!"

"Seriously, Nikki, I'm SO sorry!" Chloe apologized. "My parents said I couldn't keep the dogs anymore because my uncle is going to be here for the weekend. And, unfortunately, he says he's allergic to dogs. And just about EVERYTHING else!"

"Don't worry, Chloe. I totally understand," I assured her.

"How about Zoey? Maybe she can keep the dogs for two days?" Chloe suggested.

"I don't think so. Today is her mom's birthday, and Zoey is taking her out to dinner. They'll be gone most of the evening. So I guess I'll just keep them at my house another day." I sighed.

My stomach was already twisting into knots at the thought of hiding the dogs from my parents again.

Although I was exhausted, I felt even more sorry for Chloe.

I'd much rather spend the weekend with a pack of wild dogs than her whiny, slightly nutty, germophobic uncle Carlos.

Chloe offered to help load the dogs.

As we walked out to the van, Chloe's mom was coming in.

"Hi, Mrs. Garcia." I smiled.

"Hi, Mom," Chloe said. "And don't worry! Holly and her puppies were just leaving."

"Hi, girls! WOW! The PUPPIES are ADORABLE!" Mrs. Garcia squealed. "Well, I've got some great news for you both!"

ME, HOPING THE GREAT NEWS IS THAT
UNCLE CARLOS IS GOING HOME!!

"The Daisy Girl Scouts are having a sleepover at a neighbor's house to earn their pet care badges. So, Nikki, if it's okay with you, their troop leader, who is also my sister, would LOVE to babysit the dogs since Chloe can't do it."

"I think that's a great idea!" Chloe exclaimed. "And tomorrow, after the sleepover, Mom and I can pick up the dogs and take them to Zoey's house. I know you're exhausted and need a break, Nikki!"

Mrs. Garcia continued. "My sister loves dogs and has one of her own. So Holly and her puppies will be in good hands. And it'll be a great experience for the sixteen little girls. Who knows! You might even find a home for one of the pups."

"Actually, that sounds fantastic to me, too!" I said excitedly. "I'll just run this past Brandon to make sure it's okay with him!"

I called Brandon on my cell phone and explained the situation with Chloe's uncle and how Mrs. Garcia's sister had volunteered to watch the dogs (along with her Daisy troop). Brandon was totally sold on the idea.

So everything is all set!

Mrs. Garcia agreed to drop the dogs off at the sleepover and then drive me home.

It looks like my doggie DRAMA is over and I SURVIVED!

SQUEEEEEEEEEEEE!!!

☺!!

FRIDAY—5:15 P.M.
I CAN'T BELIEVE I'M ACTUALLY HERE!
AGAIN ☹!!

Brianna and I had fallen in love with ALL the dogs, but our favorite was the smallest puppy.

She was SUPERcute, curious, and smart, and loved to play with Brianna's stuffed animals.

Although I was really going to miss taking care of the dogs, I felt proud I had been able to help keep them safe.

I also learned that puppies can be as rambunctious as they are CUTE.

Calling Holly's seven puppies a handful was an understatement.

They were like seven tiny Tasmanian devils with puppy breath and no potty-training skills whatsoever.

I was already looking forward to seeing them at Fuzzy Friends next week.

Anyway, Chloe and I had no idea where the sleepover was going to be. But as soon as Mrs. Garcia pulled into the driveway, Chloe and I instantly recognized the house.

At first we totally FREAKED.

Then we stared in shock.

Soon we started to snicker.

And then we giggled.

Finally we laughed until our sides hurt!

Between the eight dogs and the sixteen Daisy Girl Scouts (including MY bratty little sister, Brianna), we felt really, really sorry for . . .

MACKENZIE HOLLISTER!! . . .

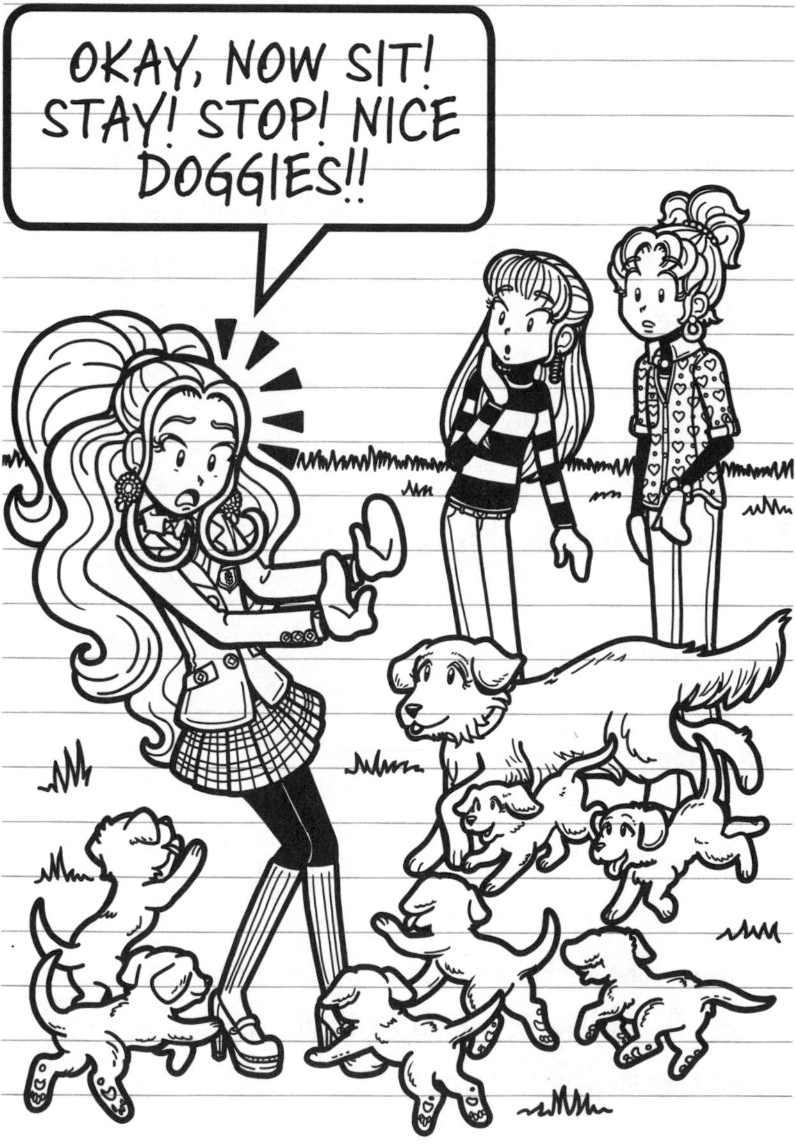
OKAY, NOW SIT! STAY! STOP! NICE DOGGIES!!

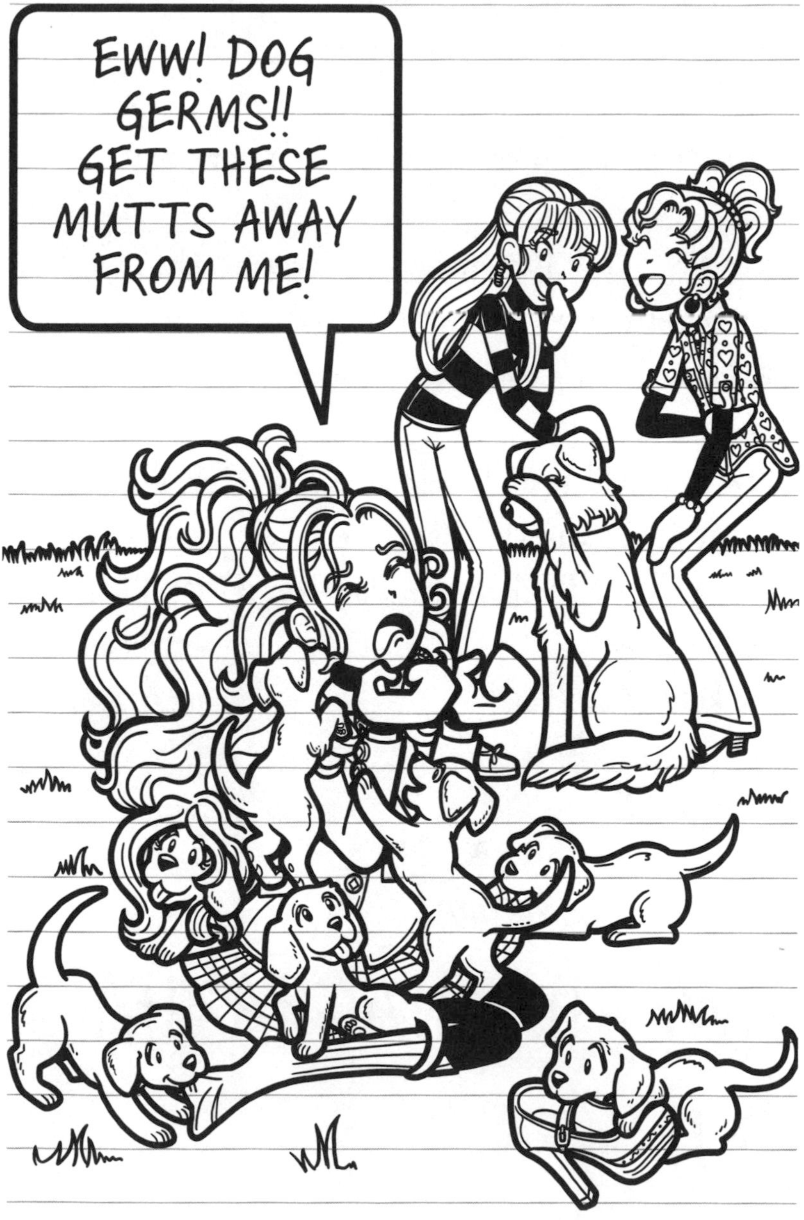
EWW! DOG GERMS!! GET THESE MUTTS AWAY FROM ME!

Sorry, but MacKenzie totally deserved every fun-filled ~~puppy~~ poopy moment!

It was going to be one VERY, VERY long night.

Especially after I suggested to Brianna that Miss Bri-Bri open a new PAW SPA right inside MacKenzie's very huge and luxurious bedroom!

Then she could provide her peanut butter facials to MacKenzie's little sister, Amanda, the fourteen other girls, AND the seven dogs for FREE!

Just kidding ☺!!

NOT!!

I am such an evil GENIUS!

MWA-HA-HA-HA-HA!

☺!!

I was so exhausted from taking care of the dogs that I slept past breakfast and lunch.

And by the time I came downstairs to grab a bite to eat, Brianna had gotten home from her sleepover and left the house again to go to ballet practice.

Which meant I hadn't gotten a chance to talk to her all day.

I was absolutely DYING to know how everything went with the puppies. And her new PAW SPA ☺!

Mom told me Brianna really enjoyed the sleepover and taking care of the puppies. And she had earned a pet care badge, which meant she'd be a responsibl(pet owner.

Anyway, I decided to ride with Mom to pick up Brianna from ballet practice.

And when I went inside to get my sister, I heard some very SCANDALOUS news!

But first let me make one thing perfectly clear.

I'm definitely not the type who spreads nasty RUMORS about other people.

And I refuse to GOSSIP behind a person's back (unlike most of the CCPs—the Cute, Cool & Popular kids—who will gossip about you right to your FACE).

But I couldn't RESIST getting the latest DIRT on a certain diary-stealing drama queen who had just transferred to North Hampton Hills International Academy.

And it came from a VERY reliable source.

Namely, MacKenzie's little sister, AMANDA.

I was just minding my own business and trying to be friendly when I said . . .

ME, TALKING TO MACKENZIE'S
LITTLE SISTER, AMANDA!

"Well, Amanda, if it's a secret, then you don't have to tell me," I said, giving her a reassuring hug. "But I'm VERY sure Santa is going to bring YOU and your BFF, Brianna, lots of fun toys this year because you're the sweetest LITTLE sister a BIG sister could EVER have!!" I ~~tied~~ gushed.

"You really think so?!" Amanda giggled. "Okay, so the big secret about MacKenzie is—"

"Wait a minute!" Brianna interrupted, smiling at me like a snake in a pink tutu. "Since we're both such sweet little sisters, will you take Amanda and me to see *Princess Sugar Plum Saves Baby Unicorn Island, Part 9?!* PLEEEASE?!"

"Wow! A Princess Sugar Plum Movie?! That would be AWESOME!" Amanda squealed.

I gave Brianna a dirty look.

I could NOT believe she was taking advantage of me like this.

But if I wanted to get the lowdown on MacKenzie, I didn't have a choice but to give in to Brianna's demands.

"Um, okay. But, Amanda, we have to ask your mom first," I explained. "Now, let's get back to MacKenzie's big secret, okay? So SPILL IT!"

Amanda took a deep breath and began a second time. "Well, when MacKenzie went to her new school, she—"

"Hold on!" Brianna interrupted. "We're going to need some hot, buttery popcorn at the movie."

"FINE!" I said, annoyed. "I'll get you popcorn!"

"And gummy bears, too!" Brianna added.

That little brat was milking this situation like a dairy cow.

I could NOT believe I was being so blatantly manipulated by my own GREEDY little sister!

Like, WHO does that?!!

"OKAY! And gummy bears, too!" I said through gritted teeth. "But nothing more. That's it! Do you understand?"

Brianna grinned at me like a baby shark. . . .

Nikki, you're the BEST sister EVER!!

"Now, Amanda, where were we before Brianna so RUDELY interrupted us?"

Amanda lowered her voice to a whisper.

Then she told me some of the things that had happened to MacKenzie at her new school.

OMG!

The stuff she said was
UNBELIEVABLE!

No wonder MacKenzie had been acting so weird when we saw her at the CupCakery.

I ALMOST felt SORRY for her!

Notice I said "almost."

Anyway, I have to stop writing in my diary now.

To celebrate Brianna earning her pet care badge, Mom is letting us have dinner at Crazy Burger!!

SQUEEEEEEEEE ☺!

I'm so hungry right now, I could eat one of those silly Styrofoam Crazy Burger hats, googly eyes and all!

☺!!

I just talked to Zoey on the phone an hour ago.
She told me that Chloe had dropped the dogs off
around noon, and Zoey has been having a blast
with them all day.

It seems so QUIET in MY bedroom now that the
dogs are gone. I really miss them.

Anyway, I'm still in shock about the stuff I heard
about MacKenzie today.

Apparently, her first day of school went fine and
everyone was SUPERfriendly. But her second day
was a disaster.

MacKenzie was in the bathroom when a group of the
most popular girls in the entire school came in. They
were laughing really hard about something, and she
heard them mention her name.

So MacKenzie peeked out of her stall and . . .

. . . CAUGHT THEM LAUGHING AND MAKING
FUN OF THAT VIDEO OF HER WITH
THE BUG IN HER HAIR!!

MACKENZIE WAS SO EMBARRASSED
AND HUMILIATED THAT SHE HID OUT
IN THAT BATHROOM STALL FOR THREE HOURS,
UNTIL SCHOOL WAS OVER!!

And then she ended up with a one-hour after-school detention for skipping class!!

Amanda said MacKenzie HATED the popular kids at North Hampton Hills because they were mean, snobby, and made fun of her because of the bug video.

OMG! All of that mean-girl drama sounded uncomfortably familiar. MacKenzie was being treated by those North Hampton Hills girls EXACTLY the same way SHE treated ME!

Apparently, some of the kids at her new school had labeled MacKenzie Hollister, THE former Queen Bee of the CCPs . . .

A BIG DORK!

Well, MacKenzie, welcome to the club ☺!

All of this is just SO unbelievably, um . . .

UNBELIEVABLE!!

Because this sounded NOTHING like the CCP MEAN GIRL who'd had a locker next to mine for eight very long months at WCD.

Come on! WHO in their right mind WOULDN'T love attending a swanky school like North Hampton Hills International Academy?!

But Amanda said MacKenzie made up cool stuff about her life and pretended to be someone else so the students there would like her. Which also explains why she had all but stolen MY identity when I met some of her friends at the CupCakery.

Anyway, my conversation with Amanda was very RUDELY interrupted by a loud, shrill voice.

"AMANDA!! I told you to NEVER talk to that little BRAT or her PATHETIC sister again! Let's go! NOW!!" MacKenzie shrieked.

Then she swooped in like a vicious . . . um, vulture, and dragged Amanda away like a . . . dead carcass. . . .

MACKENZIE GRABS AMANDA
AND DRAGS HER AWAY!

That's when a smile slowly spread across Brianna's face.

"It looks like MacKenzie is still mad about the Paw Spa I set up in her bedroom during our sleepover!" Brianna giggled. "Everybody LOVED it! Except MacKenzie."

And get this! MacKenzie didn't say a single word to me!!

She just sashayed away with her nose stuck in the air like I didn't even exist.

I just HATE it when that girl sashays!!

Anyway, it's partially Brianna's fault that I didn't get even more details about what happened. Amanda couldn't complete a full sentence without Brianna rudely interrupting to demand assorted unhealthy movie snacks.

So if I want to get more DIRT on MacKenzie, it looks like I might actually have to spend an afternoon taking Brianna and Amanda to Princess Sugar Plum Saves Baby Unicorn Island, Part 9.

Suffering through yet another of those silly, mind-numbing Princess Sugar Plum movies would be worth it just to stay one step ahead of MacKenzie and her DRAMAFEST.

☺!!

SUNDAY, MAY 4—7:00 P.M.
AT HOME

Brandon called me earlier today with some really great news about Fuzzy Friends!

According to the manager, four dogs had been picked up for adoption on Friday and six on Saturday.

So as of this morning, Fuzzy Friends had ten openings for new animals!!

SQUEEEEEEEE ☺!!!

Which meant that there was FINALLY enough space for Holly and her seven puppies!

But this is the crazy part!

ALL THE PUPPIES HAVE ALREADY BEEN ADOPTED!!! AND HOLLY, TOO!!

The vet said Holly had pretty much weaned her puppies and they were eating solid puppy food.

I felt really happy and sad at the same time! I would have LOVED to have gotten a dog of my own.

But after my mom made such a big fuss about her new furniture and carpet, I didn't even bother to ask.

Mrs. Garcia's sister adopted Holly, and FOUR puppies were adopted by the girls at the pet care sleepover! WOW!!

So thanks to Chloe's uncle Carlos, five dogs found homes!

And Marcy got a puppy, and two puppies went to people on the Fuzzy Friends waiting list for golden retrievers.

I felt a little heartbroken knowing those wonderful dogs had been placed with OTHER families.

I guess MY family would NEVER, EVER get a dog!

I couldn't help but blink back tears.

I know it's crazy to have grown so attached to them after just a few days.

But I feel depressed looking at the outline in the carpet where their cage used to be.

My room is so quiet now, I can barely sleep at all!

Brianna has been missing the puppies too.

Even though I made her swear on her Princess Sugar Plum Pink Baby Unicorn to keep the puppies a BIG SECRET, lately it's been the ONLY thing she talks about.

"You know who'd really LOVE these meatballs?" she sighed sadly at the dinner table earlier today. "Holly and her seven little puppies that we hid in Nikki's room! I really miss them."

One part of me wanted to reach across the table and slap her. And the other part of me was so freaked out that I choked on a meatball.

Well, actually . . . ALL of me was choking on that meatball!

"Nikki!" Mom cried. "Are you okay?!"

I coughed and quickly guzzled my glass of punch to wash the meatball down before my face turned blue.

"Sorry about that! These meatballs are so delicious, I'm literally trying to inhale them!" I giggled nervously.

Mom and Dad traded glances with each other.

"Now, what were you saying about puppies?" Dad asked Brianna curiously.

"Hey, Brianna!" I interrupted, trying desperately to change the subject. "How is Oliver doing? I bet he really likes meatballs too!"

"He LOVES puppies MORE!" she said glumly. "He said he wanted to play with the puppies you had in your room."

Dad furrowed his brow. "So, are these Princess Sugar Plum stuffed puppies?"

"No, Dad! They're Nikki's puppies! And they are REAL!" Brianna corrected him.

"Actually, Dad, the puppies aren't real," I explained. "But Brianna likes to pretend they live in my bedroom."

"Nuh-uh!!" she protested. "They're real and you know it! Remember the torn-up pillows in the family room? And the peanut butter and mud from the Paw Spa in the upstairs bathroom? And the dog poop in Mommy and Daddy's room? And the—"

"HA! HA! HA!" I roared over the sound of her snitching on me. "Dogs pooping in Mom and Dad's room?! OMG! You're HILARIOUS, Brianna!"

"You weren't laughing when you were lying on the middle of the bathroom floor, covered with mud, peanut butter, and toilet water!" she yelled, and stuck her tongue out at me.

"Brianna!" Mom scolded her. "That's enough!"

I could NOT believe that little BRAT was putting all of my personal business in the streets like that!

Thanks a million, Brianna!

Just throw me under the bus so Mom and Dad will ground me until my eighteenth birthday.

"I don't have the slightest idea WHY Brianna has suddenly been so obsessed with puppies lately," I shrugged, all innocentlike. "Maybe it was that pet care sleepover."

Dad and Mom exchanged glances again.

Actually, I was starting to feel a little uneasy.

I couldn't help but notice that my parents were acting kind of weird too.

Did they actually believe Brianna's crazy story?

"Nikki, after dinner I'd like you to help me bring in some groceries from the car, okay?" Mom said.

Twenty minutes later, I was carrying in a half dozen bags from Pets-N-Stuff.

"These are groceries?" I asked skeptically. "Mom, I know you've caught Brianna drinking out of the toilet and biting the mailman once or twice! But feeding her Doggy Diner puppy chow is a bit drastic, don't you think?!"

"It's a pet food drive for Brianna's troop," Mom said.

"Hey! What's this stuff?" Brianna asked. "Mom, did you buy me some puppy chow cereal? YUM!"

I couldn't believe Brianna actually said that.

"I ate lots of bacon doggie snacks when Nikki babysat me and the puppies," she bragged.

Then Dad came downstairs, carrying a big white box with a huge red bow on it.

"WOW!" I gasped. Was it a new laptop computer to replace the one Brianna had put in the dishwasher?

GIRLS! WE HAVE A BIG SURPRISE FOR YOU!

We opened the box and peeked inside!! . . .

The wiggly little puppy jumped into our arms and licked our faces.

It was Holly's smallest pup! The one that Brianna and I had fallen in love with!

"SQUEEEEEEEEEEEEEEEEEE!!" we both squealed.

"YIP! YIP! YIP! YIP!" the puppy barked.

We were SO happy, we both started to CRY!

"I've been begging your mom for a dog for a long time now, and she finally gave in!" Dad boasted. "You girls can thank me later!"

"Well, both of you have been talking about dogs nonstop all week. It made me seriously consider getting one. And when I picked up Brianna from her sleepover and saw THIS little puppy! I couldn't help but fall in love with her. I called Fuzzy Friends right away and arranged to adopt her!"

"Can we call her DAISY?!" Brianna asked excitedly. "She's the littlest, cutest, most sweetest dog in the entire world!"

I totally agreed. We were so happy and excited that we did a group hug! With DAISY! . . .

THE MAXWELL FAMILY'S NEW PUPPY!!

"Something told me she was the right dog!" Mom said, winking at Dad.

A wave of paranoia swept over me. Now, what did THAT little comment mean?!

I thought I had just gotten away with the biggest doggie-smuggling operation in Maxwell family history!

But now I was starting to wonder if it was Mom and Dad who'd pulled a fast one on Brianna and me.

Anyway, Holly and her pups had new homes!

WE had an adorable new puppy named Daisy!

And my next week at school was going to be DRAMA FREE for the first time all year!!

My life was PERFECT ☺!!

Until I got a copy of a parent e-mail from Principal Winston. . . .

TO: Mr. and Mrs. Maxwell

FROM: Principal Winston

RE: Eighth-Grade Student Exchange Week

Dear Parents,

Each year, all eighth-grade students at WCD Middle School participate in a Student Exchange Week with local schools. We feel this helps to foster community and good citizenship with both students and faculty at the host schools.

Your child, Nikki Maxwell, will be attending NORTH HAMPTON HILLS INTERNATIONAL ACADEMY along with several other WCD students. Everyone is expected to be on their best behavior, to follow the student handbook of the host school, and to make WDC proud. More information about this very important event will be sent home with students next week. If you have any questions or concerns, please feel free to contact me.

Sincerely,
Principal Winston

At first I thought the letter was some kind of PRANK. But when I checked the WCD calendar on our school website, sure enough, the Student Exchange Week was listed as an official event.

JUST GREAT ☹!!

So now I'm going to be attending school with MacKenzie Hollister?!!

Just when I thought that drama queen was out of my life FOREVER, she shows up AGAIN like a recurring NIGHTMARE!

Although, from what I've heard, I think she could probably use my help! Hey, it's really TOUGH when other kids make you feel like an outsider.

But you just have to believe in YOURSELF!! How do I know this? Probably because . . .

I'M SUCH A DORK!
☺!!

Want to see more of
Brandon and Nikki's new friend
Max Crumbly?

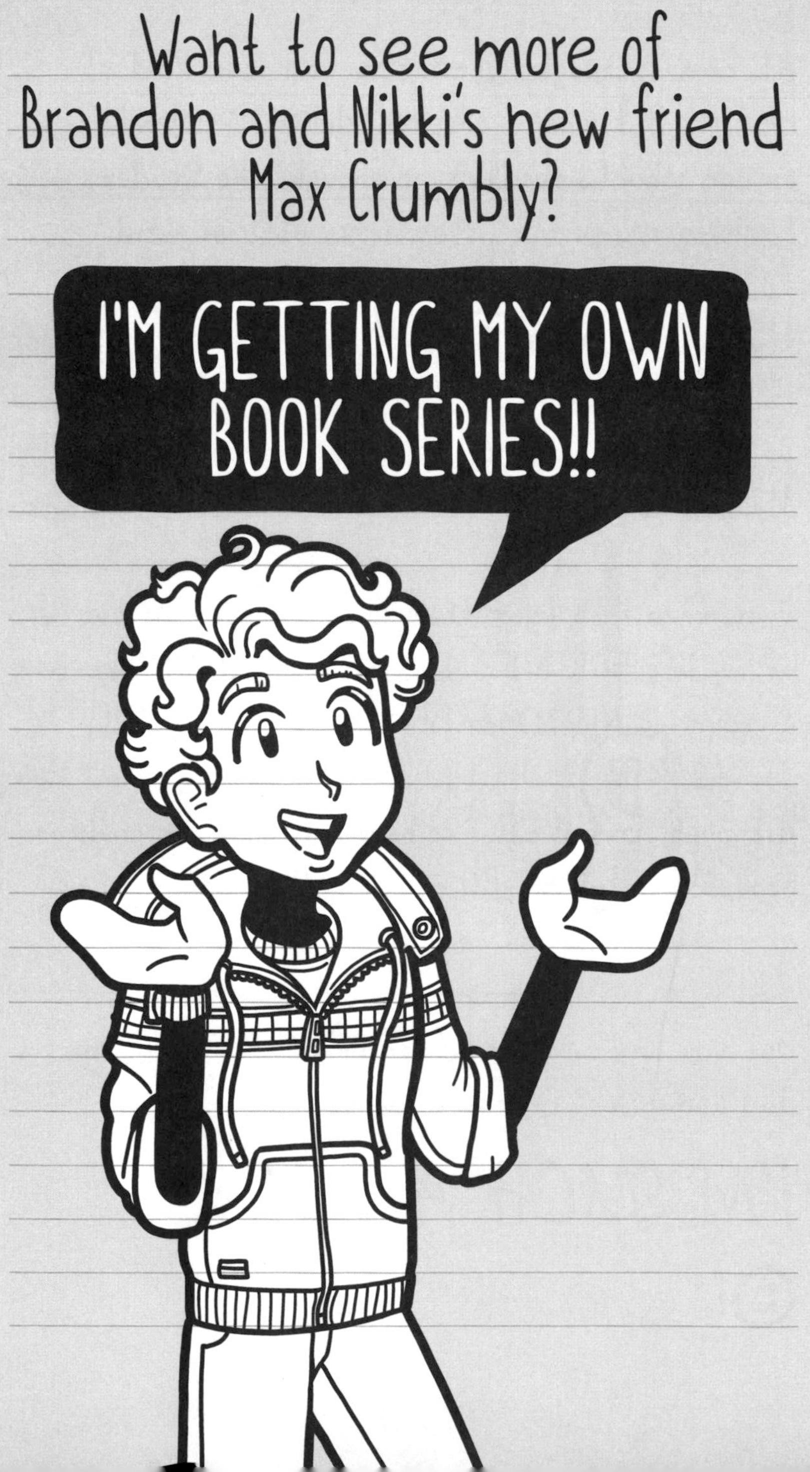
I'M GETTING MY OWN BOOK SERIES!!

NEXT SPRING,
LOOK OUT FOR . . .

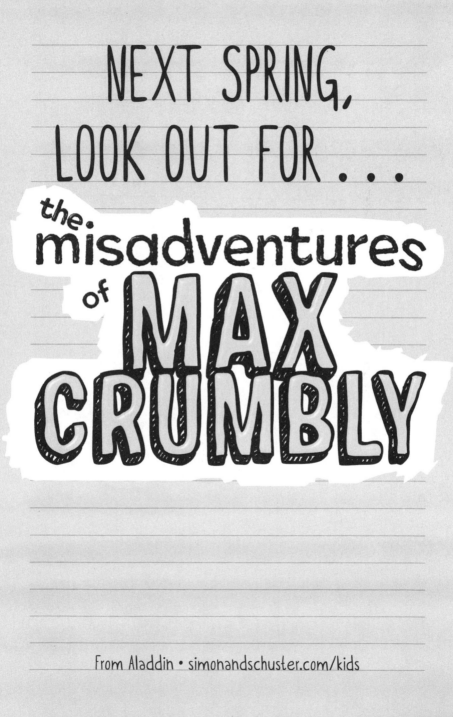

the misadventures of MAX CRUMBLY

From Aladdin • simonandschuster.com/kids

Turn the page for a couple of
my favorite tips on keeping a diary,
from *Dork Diaries 3½*:

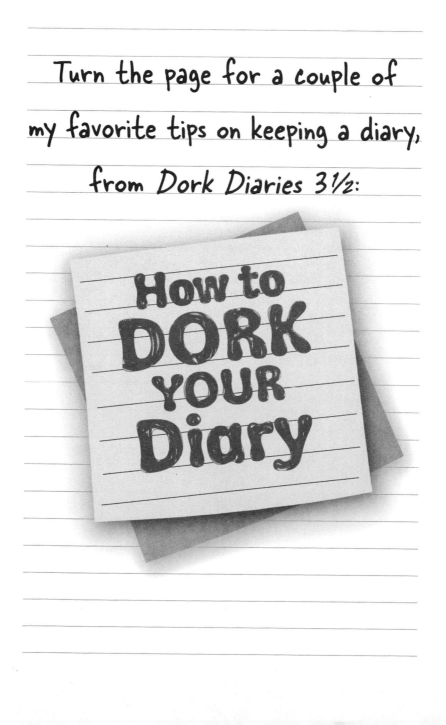

NOTE TO SELF

WARNING:

Unfortunately, parents, bratty kid sisters and brothers, friends, enemies, and even total strangers LOVE to read diaries that do NOT belong to them.

HOW TO DORK YOUR DIARY TIP #1

NEVER, EVER LEAVE YOUR DIARY WHERE A NOSY CREEP CAN SNEAK A PEEK!

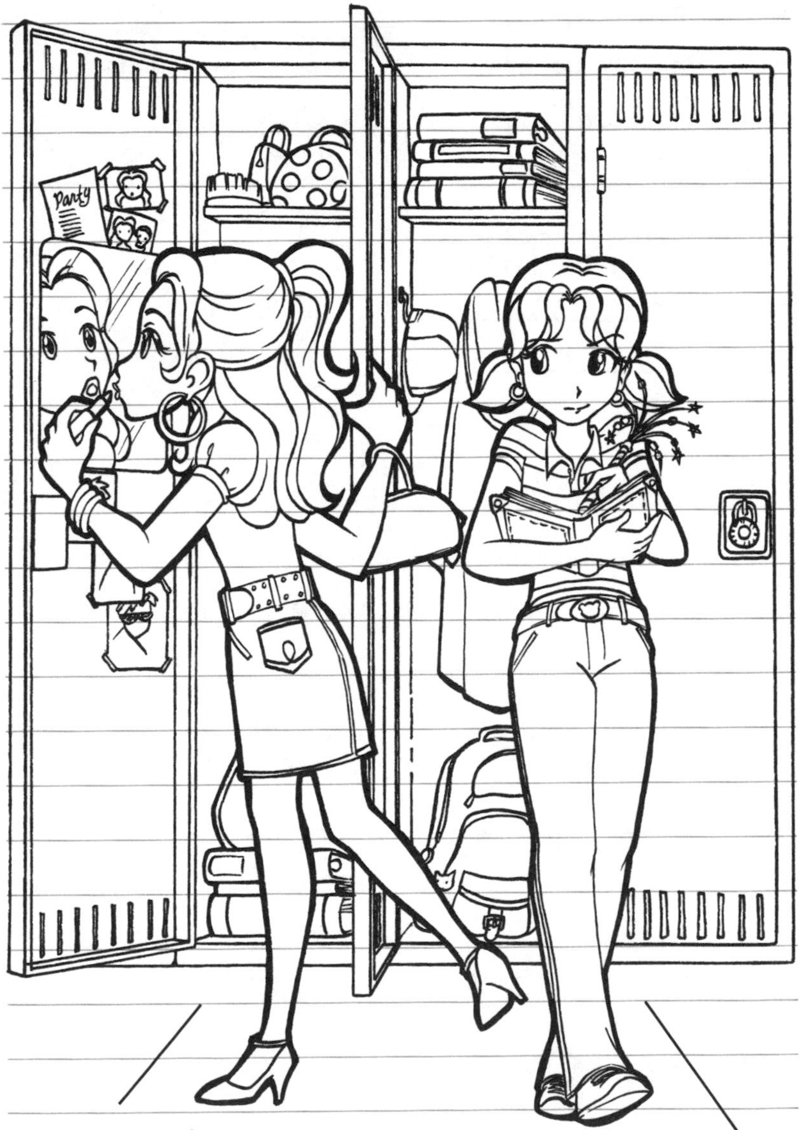

OMG, NIKKI!
YOU'RE WRITING
IN A DIARY?
CAN I READ IT?

OH, THIS? IT'S JUST A . . . BOOK
I GOT FROM MY DOCTOR ON, UM . . .
TOENAIL ODOR.

If someone caught you writing in your diary, what would you say to trick them? Write four different responses below:

HEY! IS THAT YOUR DIARY?!

Never let anyone tell you that keeping a diary is a silly or childish thing to do. Reflecting on your feelings and experiences is actually a very mature activity. If someone said something rude about you having a diary, what would your response be?

ONLY DORKS HAVE DIARIES!

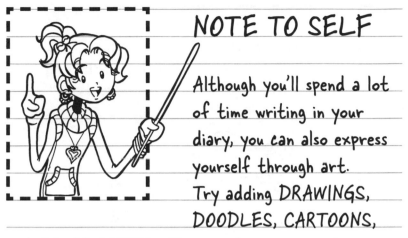

NOTE TO SELF

Although you'll spend a lot of time writing in your diary, you can also express yourself through art.
Try adding DRAWINGS, DOODLES, CARTOONS, and COMIC STRIPS. They can be serious, artsy, emo, or just plain silly. If you're a supertalented artist, create a masterpiece. Or try drawing simple stick people. Or trace your hand and make it into a turkey like you did back in kindergarten. Just have FUN!

HOW TO DORK YOUR DIARY TIP #2

RELEASE YOUR INNER ARTIST!

Here is a four-panel comic strip called "My Diary Drama." (A panel is just another name for the box the artwork is placed inside.)

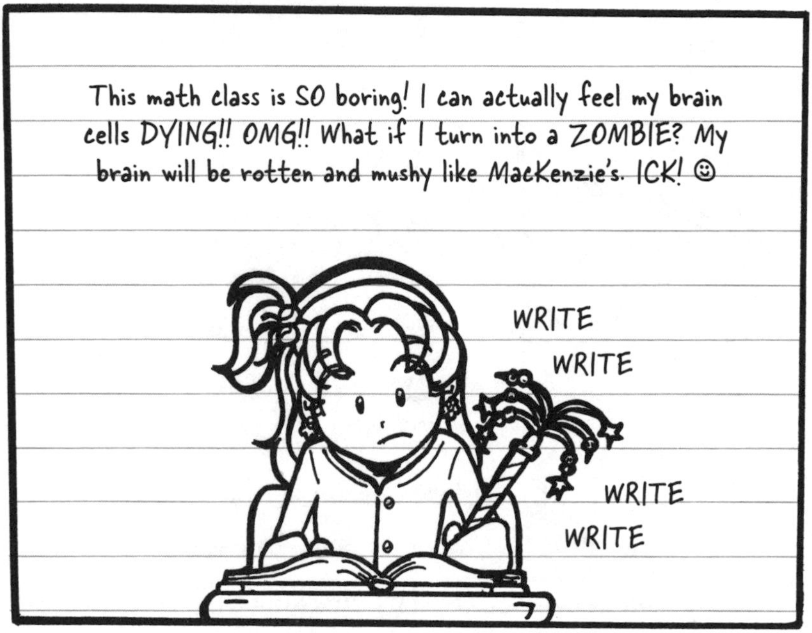
This math class is SO boring! I can actually feel my brain cells DYING!! OMG!! What if I turn into a ZOMBIE? My brain will be rotten and mushy like MacKenzie's. ICK! ☺
WRITE
WRITE
WRITE
WRITE

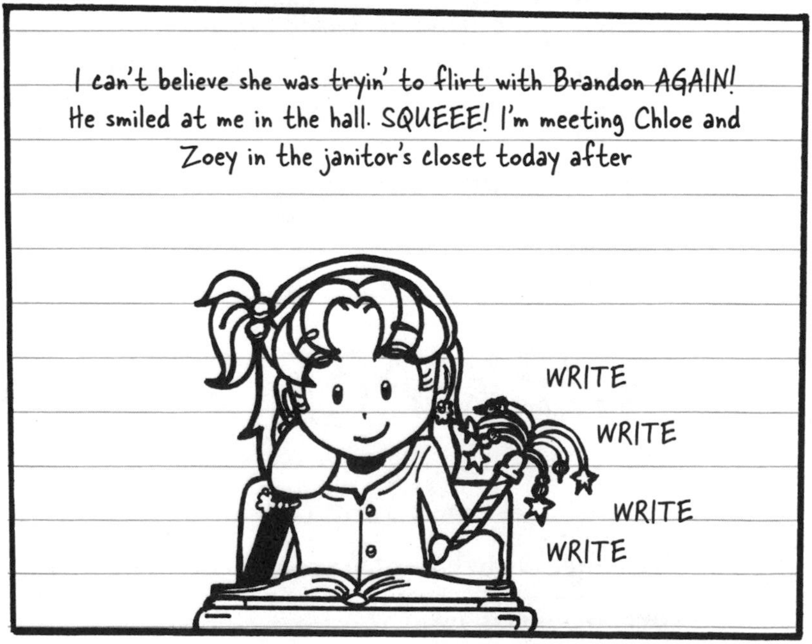
I can't believe she was tryin' to flirt with Brandon AGAIN! He smiled at me in the hall. SQUEEE! I'm meeting Chloe and Zoey in the janitor's closet today after
WRITE
WRITE
WRITE
WRITE

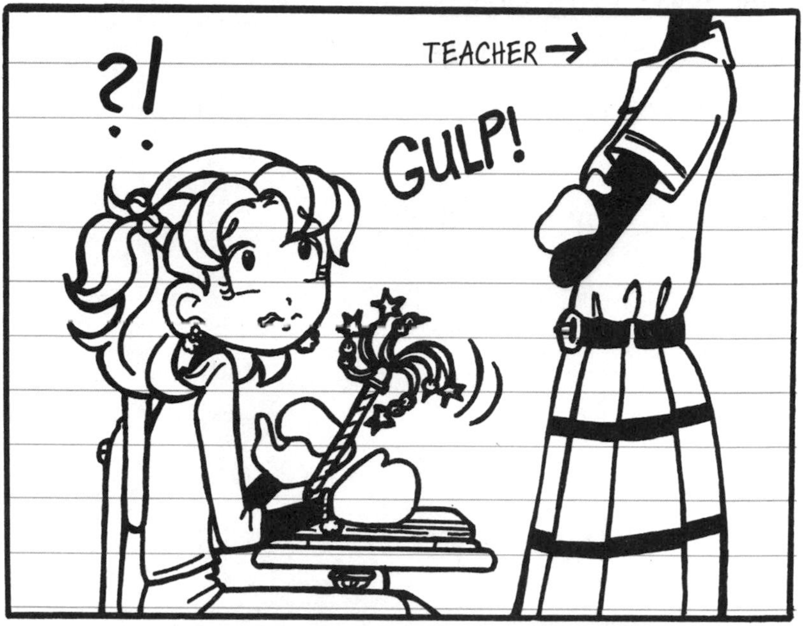
?!
TEACHER →
GULP!

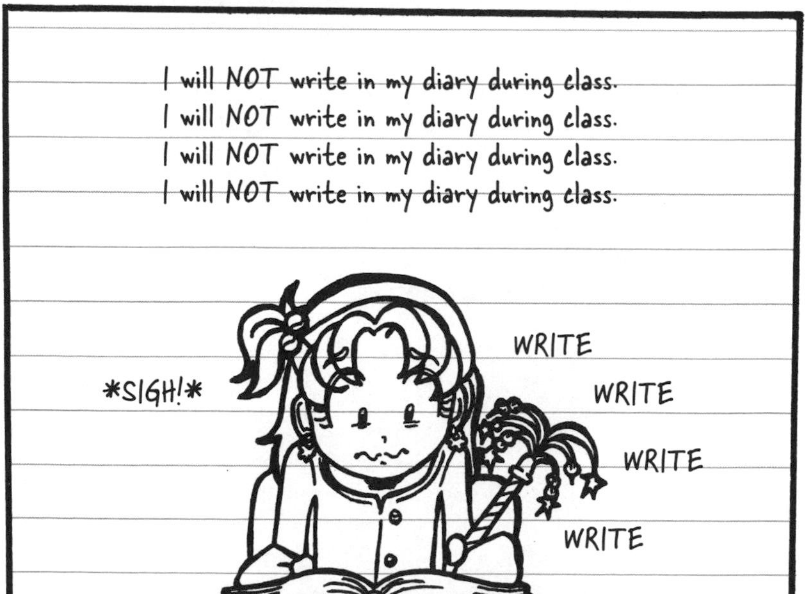
I will NOT write in my diary during class.
I will NOT write in my diary during class.
I will NOT write in my diary during class.
I will NOT write in my diary during class.
SIGH!
WRITE
WRITE
WRITE
WRITE

Now you're going to make your own four-panel comic strip! But before you get started, plan what it is going to be about.

My comic strip is called:

PANEL 1
Panel 1 will contain a picture of:

The characters are saying:

PANEL 2

Panel 2 will contain a picture of:

_____

_____

_____

_____

_____

_____

The characters are saying:

_____

_____

_____

_____

_____

_____

PANEL 3

Panel 3 will contain a picture of:

_____

_____

_____

_____

_____

The characters are saying:

_____

_____

_____

_____

_____

PANEL 4

Panel 4 will contain a picture of:

_____

_____

_____

_____

_____

The characters are saying:

_____

_____

_____

_____

_____

Now you're ready to draw your own comic strip in
the space provided. Have fun ☺!

DISCOVER YOUR DIARY IDENTITY.

OMG, my worst nightmare came true—
I lost my diary!!
What if MacKenzie finds it before I do??
Chloe and Zoey are helping me search,
so I'm going to help YOU by sharing all of my tips
on how to keep a Dorky Diary!

From Aladdin • simonandschuster.com/kids

Rachel Renée Russell is an attorney who prefers writing tween books to legal briefs. (Mainly because books are a lot more fun and pajamas and bunny slippers aren't allowed in court.)

She has raised two daughters and lived to tell about it. Her hobbies include growing purple flowers and doing totally useless crafts (like, for example, making a microwave oven out of Popsicle sticks, glue, and glitter). Rachel lives in northern Virginia with a spoiled pet Yorkie who terrorizes her daily by climbing on top of a computer cabinet and pelting her with stuffed animals while she writes. And, yes, Rachel considers herself a total Dork.